Outermark

Outermark

A Novel

JASON BROWN

PAUL DRY BOOKS
Philadelphia 2024

First Paul Dry Books Edition, 2024

Paul Dry Books, Inc.
Philadelphia, Pennsylvania
www.pauldrybooks.com

Printed in the United States of America

Library of Congress Control Number: 2024939887
ISBN: 978-1-58988-194-5

Table of Contents

for Nicola and Isabella

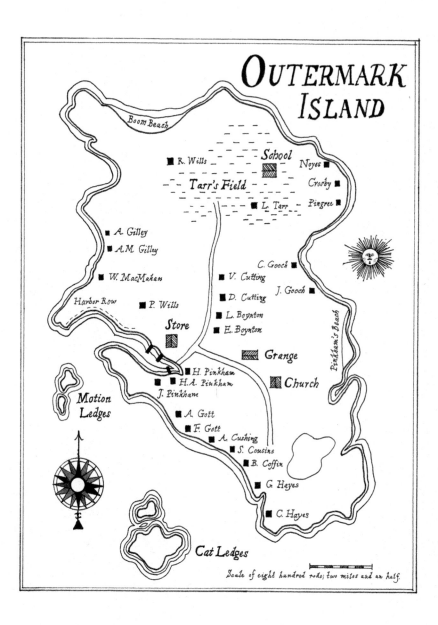

Corson's Story
2022

"VOICES FROM THE PAST," the file is called, "An Archive of Local Stories." When they first asked me to be part of this project, I explained that I knew little about Carleton, where we all live. For forty years or so, I've cycled from my home to my job at the library without getting too entangled. The high school kids setting up the archive said that they wanted to know about my life on the island before I moved to Carleton. My response was to ask why. Assuming that people in the future could even read, which I thought was assuming a lot, I couldn't see why anyone would want to read about the island where I'd grown up. It's far away—from everything. It's a rock in the ocean where no one lives anymore.

At first, I couldn't figure out how these kids had even heard about the island, but the answer to that question was my old friend Janet. She still volunteered in the schools. Having somehow heard that I'd scared the kids away, Janet called me and asked that I reconsider. The project was organized by a teacher she knew. Janet also reminded me that this town had accepted me and my grandparents when we moved here in 1980. I'm not sure what I owe the town of Carleton, if anything (I spent more than a few afternoons after school in my first years having my face smashed into snowbanks by the children of iron workers), and I have good reasons for not wanting to talk about my family and the island. In the end I agreed because Janet asked. Janet and I worked at the library together for many years. I doubt I would even be here if it were not for her.

So, I'll begin. My name is Corson Wills. The 750-acre island where I grew up is shaped like the kind of heart that sits in your chest. In 1980 there were about forty people living there, depending on the time of year. A few, like a man we called Christopher Columbus, an MIT drop-out, lived there in the summer only. He spent most of his time painting pictures of rotting boats and barnacles, but if you needed him to fix an engine, he was always willing to help. Christopher was from Massachusetts somewhere. Just about everyone else on Outermark had been there forever. My family, the Wills family, came in the 1720s along with the Cushings and the Pinkhams. Jacob, our teacher the year I was twelve, his mother's family, the Mac-Neils, arrived sometime in the 1800s from Cape Breton. No one who wasn't from there visited us, and, except for my grandfather who picked up the mail and groceries, those of us who lived there rarely made the thirty-mile trip to Dennis on the mainland.

The harbor faced west toward the mainland, and I spent many nights there watching the bridge lights of tankers rising over swells. The horizon was usually black except for the Machias Seal Island Light flashing thirteen miles west. I used to think of some Canadian guardsman on Machias Seal lying awake looking at Gannet Light flashing eleven miles farther west on Grand Manan Island, and on Grand Manan someone else looking ten miles farther still to Quoddy Head Light in the State of Maine.

The summer before we left the island I lived most of the time at the harbor with my mother's parents. My mother lived in the middle of the island with Jacob, who'd been born on the island but had lived away for twenty years. He'd just come back six months before, and he and my mother had started in together almost right away. I didn't stay at my grandparents' house because I minded Jacob living with my mother. In fact, I wanted to spend all the time with him that I could—just not around him and my mother together. I had this idea that he would train me to be a surveyor. He'd been a surveyor for oil companies all over the world before coming back to the island. I dreamed that I would leave the island as my ship captain ancestors had and make a fortune in some distant land. Only when I was rich would I return and rebuild my grandmother's store.

The harbor was shaped like a horseshoe. The guy who lived across the harbor from us, a fisherman named Gus Pinkham, was the highliner, the best fisherman, but you wouldn't know it to look at his gear—rotting traps everywhere, coils of rope mixed with old bait and what not. He was always dressed in agony, as my grandmother used to say, with bait smeared over his sweatshirt. My whole childhood I remember falling asleep listening to his unlatched storm door banging against the side of his house. That's how I knew the wind was coming up. In the fall and winter, the door banged harder. It was like living on a mountain peak. Even in the middle of the island there was barely enough soil to burry a potato. People who lived around the harbor bolted their houses to the ledge with steel cables. Our house sometimes shook like a ship in a storm and pulled against those cables until they sang.

Gus's son Henry had a house and a fish shack on the harbor, too, as well as a few other people, and there was my grand-mother's store at the head of the harbor. Right in front of the store was the weir. The weir was my responsibility. My grand-father had rebuilt his father's weir by stretching netting between poles sunk in the harbor. I had kept it going because I was con-vinced it was going to pay. It was one of those things. The more

you sank into it, the more you convinced yourself it was going
to work. Over the last year, the weir had twisted into a bent half
circle that opened toward the sea. My great-grandfather had
twice filled seiners, but that was back in 1952. As my mother
liked to say, in 1980 we were just changing the water.

It's not the weir itself I want to tell you about but one of the
nights I rowed out to it to see if our luck had changed. The
wind slackened and stars floated on the surface of the harbor.
The herring only came in during a calm like this. Pushing the
oars away from my chest, I glided around the moored boats in
the punt. Once inside the walls of the weir, I leaned over the
side. Black as ink. I had to be careful on the punky bottom, so I
tapped softly to stir the fish. Nothing. Stamped my foot. Phos-
phorescent sparks spread around the scattering fins. When I
stomped again, glittering trails rolled underwater toward shore.
Not bright enough, not wide enough, I knew, but enough for
the dip net, maybe enough to wake my grandfather. I rowed to
my grandfather's wharf, climbed the ladder, and ran up the trail.
My grandparents slept in the back room, but my grandmother
kept an ear cocked like a satellite dish. As soon as my feet hit the
clamshell path, her head appeared in the window.

"What?" she demanded when I reached the kitchen. That's
the way she communicated—pounding like a rubber hammer.
"What is it?" Her elbows hung like wings off a dragger. Nothing I could say would convince her that we should all be out
of bed at this hour. When I said I'd seen fire in the water, she
frowned, lit the lamp, and shook my grandfather. He sat and
hung his head. He'd a dozen different empty stares, all of them
passing over his face as he tried to wake. Even though he'd told
me to wake him if anything stirred in the pocket, probably he
no longer meant what he'd said. For a moment, I thought he
might decide to stay in bed, but then he rested his hand on my
shoulder. He was only sixty-two, two years younger than my

grandmother, but sometimes he acted like it hurt to walk across the room. I passed him his boots and told him I'd seen no more than a few sparks.

"Just go," my grandmother said, "get it over with."

I followed in his footsteps. We took the larger, deeper dory, and my grandfather rowed while I held the dip net. My grandfather headed for the bow of his boat moored in the middle of the harbor where he hauled up a bottle he kept weighted underwater. He unscrewed the top and took a long swig. Having failed years before to make the island dry, my grandmother had settled for making her own house dry. This was the result.

The lantern would've worked, but my grandfather used rags soaked in kerosene tied to the end of a stick because the flame attracted more herring. When we reached the pocket, he struck a match and lit the torch. The sky, the harbor, the other boats moored around us, all disappeared behind a curtain of light thrown by the flames. Clumps of burning cloth dropped into the water as he held the torch over the gunwales. The herring swarmed like moths, mouths gaping. With a quick swipe, he netted and dumped them squirming into the dory. After the fifth pass, he came up empty, and I could read his mind: nothing but a lick-up, not worth getting out of bed for.

Holding the torch over the starboard side, I spotted sticks floating in the water, four separate stubs, like tiny alder trunks, pointing to the sky and turning in the current. My grandfather rowed closer until we bumped four hooves among the lobster boats. Then I saw more legs, too many to count. In a few places, sheep floated on their sides. My grandfather raised the torch higher. All around us legs pressed against the hulls of boats. As the flame dimmed, he dropped the torch into the water. I didn't say a word, but I knew only Danny could've killed all his uncle Gus's sheep.

As soon as the dory touched the ladder, I scrambled toward

the house. I didn't know what to say to my grandmother because it was my fault. That's the way I felt at the time anyway. I'd talked to Gus about his daughter, Sarah, and Danny. I'd told Gus that I'd seen them together, so Gus had shipped his daughter over to his wife's people on Grand Manan Island.

"Where's my million-dollar load of herring?" my grandmother said when she saw me.

"Danny killed the sheep," I said right away. As usual, I'd opened my mouth before I even knew what would come out. My grandmother inspired that kind of reaction in people. Her eyes pinched. In the kitchen, we looked out the window to where my grandfather loaded the herring into one of the barrels outside his fish house, and she lit the larger lamp. On a normal day, the diesel engines of half a dozen boats would fire an hour before dawn, and one at a time the fishermen would motor to their grounds. But the next day wouldn't be a normal day. My grandmother pumped water into the kettle for tea and turned to me with a snail twist in the corner of her mouth. She told me she knew I'd made up lies to tell Gus about his daughter and Danny.

I knew what I'd seen two days before when I crossed Tarr's Field in the middle of the island. At first Sarah. Then Danny, bungs up again—same thing that always happened whenever he'd more than fifty cents or something to trade for a bottle. Sarah's cheeks reddened when her hand touched Danny's hip to steady herself, and she leaned her forehead against him. I'd told Gus that I'd seen them "pressed up together." Maybe I knew what I was doing, maybe I didn't. It's hard to say now. I'd also told Gus that they were drunk. That much was true.

To escape my grandmother, I retreated to my room to crank the Wanderer with one of the records my grandfather had brought back from the war. Old wooden sea trunks in the corner contained calfskin logbooks going back two hundred years.

I lifted the lid and reached toward the bottom of the trunk, hoping to pick one I hadn't read in a while. As I listened to *cause that's the night that my sweetie and I used to dance cheek to cheek* and *I don't mind Sunday night at all 'cause that's the night friends come to call*—music that usually lifted me up but didn't at the moment—my eyes skimmed manifests: lumber, fish, brick, lime.... I followed the curves of the scrawl to Bombay, Colombo, Tranquebar, Nagapattinam, and Madras. What was the point of reading about these places if I'd never go there? I was too young to go on my own. Jacob, my teacher, had promised he would take me someday, to see some of the places he'd worked as a surveyor.

I'd been spending most of my afternoons after school with Jacob as he taught me about surveying and told me stories about other places he'd lived. Then, for no apparent reason, he had let Danny come to school. In the afternoons, Jacob started tutoring Danny, who had no interest in learning math. Danny was somewhere in his late twenties. No one knew exactly how old he was. He was a Pinkham by his mother; his father was a man named Jim no one knew, and his mother had left the island when he was young. He'd been raised by the whole island, mostly by my grandmother. Now he was a grown man. Everyone knew he was in the school to be near his cousin Sarah, who'd recently turned seventeen and overnight, it seemed, started to look like a woman.

The kitchen kettle whistled while I listened to records. Then I heard a gunshot from the other side of the island—Gus gunning for pheasants over by Boom Beach. I joined my grandmother at the kitchen window. Light had crept in around the edges of things, and we could see a dozen or more sheep floating among the buoys, gear floats, and white hulls.

"Fetch Grandpa out the bedroom, his glass," my grandmother said, and I went to find the binoculars. My grandfather pretended to sleep in bed; one of his eyelids fluttered as I passed him. My grandmother held the binoculars to her eyes and began to search the gray horizon. I knew that when Gus saw the sheep, he and his son Henry would start banging on doors with their shotguns searching for Danny.

A flock of petrels turning into the wind came to rest on my grandfather's boat, and the water, I remember, swelled like a fat tongue into the harbor and pulled back into the sea. Before long I heard the clang of Gus's truck driving the two miles from Boom Beach.

Grandma looked right at me, telling me with her eyebrows that this was all my doing. Within a few minutes, Gus pulled to a stop in front of the store. The white stars painted on the doors of his truck had started to fade, but the man behind the wheel sat high in his chariot. Constable by his own election, the King. Gus stomped along the trail to his wharf. The end of his leather belt stuck out from the buckle. His wife, Flossie, from Manan by birth, stepped out of their kitchen door and shaded her eyes, probably so she could scan the harbor for people coming to steal her carton of *Kools*. Then Gus's son, Henry, stepped out of his house, and they all came together on their wharf. Gus and Henry climbed down the ladder to their punt, and with one foot in the stern and one in the bow, Gus rocked across the harbor to his boat while he kept an eye on the shore. These were the guys who ran the place, which my grandmother hated.

"Come with me," Grandma said and pulled me along the path. "Nothing but a back porch listener. I want your hands busy, and I want you where I can see you." She pointed to the firewood, cut to the wrong length for the stove, and some not even split yet. Always something to do. Endless firewood, working on my grandfather's fishing gear, working with my grandmother in the store, hauling and scraping the boat, helping my grandmother clean or shuck clams.

"When you're finished with that, wash the salt off the windows," my grandmother said and searched the harbor. I knew my grandmother had been afraid of what Danny would do when he saw that Gus had taken Sarah to Manan. Now he was out there watching the whole show. He could duck out of your way right before you got there, then step into the place where you'd just been. Lived so long outdoors and in that leaky shack, he could move like water.

Gus tied lines around the rear legs of the dead sheep and dragged the mass of wool behind the *Flossie* to the hydraulic winch on the island wharf. I couldn't see the tendons bulging on Gus's neck where they vanished beneath his mangy beard, but I'd seen them in the past when he shaved. He scrambled up the ladder, marched across the wharf with long strides, turned on the winch, and looped the rope attached to the first sheep over the wheel. As the winch motor strained, the line shook and seemed about to snap. Gallons of water poured out of the wool, spread over the wharf, and dropped into the harbor. I tried to look away but couldn't. The small, stupid eyes of the sheep stared straight ahead. Front hooves pointed down, the mouth hung open, the tongue stuck out. People from around the island had shown up to see the awful mess. The head of one sheep dumped near the edge of the wharf swung when the rope of the next sheep coming up brushed against its nose.

Jacob showed up from the middle of the island and leaned over, breathing hard. He said my friend Ames had stopped by the school and told him what had happened. When he straightened up and saw the sheep, he cringed.

"Gus's gonna put this on me," he said. My grandmother crossed her arms over her chest and stared at Gus until he finally stopped hooking sheep and wiped his hands on his jeans, staining the denim on his thighs with two wet prints.

"Where the hell's Danny?" Gus yelled.

My grandmother set her jaw—her last word on the subject. Relations had gone downhill between my grandmother and Gus over the last year, after the fishing got worse. They had always been tense over Danny.

Ever since Gus's sister, Danny's mother, left the island when Danny was young, Gus had treated Danny like a letter from the IRS, and it had been up to my grandmother to make sure the boy had blue jeans and blackjack gingerbread on his birthdays. No one asked her to do it; no one else would've done it. Danny wasn't kin in any literal sense, but she had made him one of her own. I didn't like it. My mother and my grandfather didn't much like it, either, but that's the way it was. We had no choice. Danny was one of her boys, just as Jacob had been before he left the island when he was thirteen. Just as I was. Boys without fathers. Danny and I never knew our fathers, while Jacob's father was drunk when he could manage it. So, when Jacob first said he wanted to let Danny attend the school, my grandmother helped clean Danny up. Combed his hair. Shaved him. Nicks on his neck and chin. Now that the sheep were dead, I was sure that she blamed herself. Told herself she should've clapped both Danny and Sarah on the ears when she saw them walking together. I'd heard her say that Sarah was a stupid girl to wag her tail at him. Danny and Sarah weren't in love. There was just no one else for either of them to chase after.

Now Gus and Henry, all day bragging on the two-way about holding the line against Russian trawlers, wouldn't think twice about shipping Danny to the mainland. They'd had enough of him. The island couldn't afford a war, about Danny or anything else. It would just give people more excuses to leave. Low lobster landings, cost of diesel, now Henry running cocaine into Passamaquoddy Bay. Five families had moved off the island in the previous two years because they couldn't catch enough lobster or get enough money for what they did catch. Most guys weren't rigged for scalloping or mussels—the outlay for a season on the outside was longer than a man could hope to gain.

Gus rushed over from his wharf, and my grandmother met him on the path.

"We'll pay you for the sheep," she said and nodded at Jacob, who nodded back. My grandmother tried to convince Gus that Danny wasn't bothering anyone, but that was a hard sell. She also said the school needed Danny because of the state funding, which Gus knew wasn't the case. The state gave us money per student for the school, but no one was counting Danny. Her general point was true. If we lost the school, more people would leave the island. No school, no store, no taxes—no government funding for my grandfather's contract to pick up mail from the Main. That would be it.

Gus turned to Jacob and said, "We didn't have this trouble with Danny since a long time before you got here."

This statement wasn't true, but Gus believed it. Until six months before, Jacob had been gone from the island for twenty years, and now Gus and Henry saw him as someone from nowhere.

"You *don't* know what Corson saw between Sarah and Danny," my grandmother said. "You can't settle this on something the boy told you."

I didn't like being called "the boy," but I wasn't about to draw attention to myself.

Gus reported that Sarah had been coming home drunk. He knew she was getting it from Danny.

"I'm not keeping my daughter over on Manan forever. I want Danny *gone*. And *you*." Gus jammed his finger in Jacob's direction. "You're no teacher. A scout for oil companies. You don't belong out here anymore than your father did. I don't know but Donna's been right to lead Danny around—I don't care, tell the truth. Goddamned kid's sainted to Donna, but why do you give a shit about Danny or any of us? You must've really pooched your life out there to want to come back here."

Jacob said he was going to look for Danny and would stop by my grandmother's later.

Jacob's father, Everett, who'd drowned himself in the harbor two years before, had been from the mainland, but his mother's people had lived with Gus's people for several hundred years. That didn't seem to matter. Everett had moved to the island and worked as a sternman after he married Jacob's mother, but no one really accepted him. According to tradition, the women from Outermark married men from Manan, a larger island close to the mainland, and the women from Manan married men from Outermark, but men from elsewhere rarely moved to the island. I can't think of one other example in my memory. As soon as Jacob's mother took Jacob and moved them out west somewhere, everyone expected Jacob's father to go back to the mainland, but he stayed and worked whenever he could. It was a shock when he drowned himself, particularly to my grand-mother. She'd fed him kitchen scraps over the years, but when it came to work, he had a reputation for getting things done in the time of it. She always turned him away.

In the last few years, my grandmother had started to seem both unbreakable and brittle at the same time, like the bare branches of an oak. In the old days, she'd run the school com-mittee, the harbor committee—that convinced the state to build the government wharf—the tax committee, the charge committee. She formed a group of women who wanted the island to go dry. That's when the Pinkhams and other lobster-men took her posts away and elected Gus island constable and dog patrol. All other positions were more or less eliminated. They had the numbers, they had the votes. "You people," she told them at the time, "don't even know how to use outhouses." Lem, Gus's father, was known for shitting on a *Bangor Daily* and shoving it in the woodstove; his kids for delivering the goods off the edge of the wharf into the harbor right next to the lobster cars holding that morning's catch, not twelve hours from sitting on someone's table in Boston. My grandmother liked to say that she'd never once been forced to eat a lobster—no more than she'd been forced to eat a seagull.

We'd been having the same arguments, more or less, for generations. My family was from one of the old shipping families. At one time we'd been captains of ships running up and down the coast and all the way to India. The island had 250 people or more then, and two stores, both owned by my family, that served ships headed out to the Banks. The sea lanes were the highways and the islands main street to all commerce. The Pinkhams had always been shore huggers, peapod lobstermen and net haulers running credit in my family's ledgers until they saw their chance with the dry out and smuggled whiskey in from Canada. My grandmother liked to remind Gus of where he'd come from.

After my grandmother got done talking to Gus, she sent me to find Jacob and help him look for Danny. She was afraid Gus and Henry would find him first. I spotted Jacob heading across Tarr's Field in the middle of the island and thought I could get him to forget about Danny for a minute. This might be our last day before the freeze; maybe he'd want to take a walk or go fishing off the beach. I wanted to prove I was smart—smarter, even, than my mother—and quick with numbers the way you had to be as a surveyor's assistant.

All the kids in the school—just the dozen of us—wanted to spend time with Jacob. We were used to having new teachers, all of them young women, come through every few years. With most of our new teachers, one of the kids usually would stick a rag in the stovepipe come fall so the schoolhouse would fill up with smoke and we could all go home. No one had done this to Jacob yet because he sounded like the NOAA man, the radio

announcer for the National Oceanic and Atmospheric Asso-
ciation, who pronounced every letter in every word and every
word in every sentence as he delivered confident updates on the
results of atmospheric pressure that meant nothing at all.

"Where do you think Danny is?" Jacob asked me when I ran
up to him. His brow bunched like a dishrag. You didn't find
Danny. At some point, he would rise for air like a porpoise. To
our right, Henry appeared following the tree line with his shotgun pointed at the ground. I touched Jacob on the arm. The sky
had dunned over; only a bit of light remained around the edge
of things. The empty horizon to the east had turned the blue-
gray of fish scales the way it did in the fall at this time of day.

"Hurry, down to the beach before Henry gets there," Jacob
said.

I ran after Jacob but could barely keep up with his long
strides. Swinging the barrel of his gun, Henry dipped into the
trees.

"Where's he going?" Jacob asked.

"Pinkham Beach," I said.

"Danny wouldn't go there. That makes no sense."

Danny, sense like the wind, as my grandfather said. At least
Henry was out of sight. A southerly breeze had taken the bite
out of the air, and the Boom Beach surf washing through the
fist-sized beach stones sounded, I imagined, like the clapping
hooves of Napoleon's cavalry chasing the Austrians out of Lom-
bardy. *Britannica,* Volume 19: Mun-Oddfellows. I was reading
from start to finish through my grandmother's whole Britannica
set.

"Come on, we have to find Danny," Jacob said and kept walking. He stepped over the stones until he reached the sand. At
the end of the beach, a dead seal, half-buried with part of its
head missing, pulled him up short. A hollow looked out where
an eye would've been; a mound of clay sat in its open skull.

Because seals stole from their traps, fishermen from the island shot them without a second thought.

———

I don't know what I was thinking when I started this. I set out to provide the kind of history you read on a computer file in the library to get a feeling for what life was like in the distant past, but I have never been distant from any of this. If anything, the older I get, the closer I am to this time. The closer I get, the less I know what to say, particularly about what happened next.

When Jacob and I gave up looking for Danny, I returned to my grandmother's and sat by my bedroom window and watched the harbor. I had hoped that Jacob would come to supper at my grandmother's. He usually did when my mother was away diving with the sea urchin boat from Manan. My grandmother gave me two cookies for doing the dishes, which meant she thought she had won her argument with Gus, and Danny would be able to stay on the island. Jacob would spend every afternoon helping him with his geometry homework. I remember that the whole situation with Danny had me haired up. Here we were, all thinking about him. That's what he wanted.

Sometime past ten, the sound of snoring filled the house, and I slipped out. Taking up my perch on a crate in front of my grandfather's fish house, I watched black clouds roll in from the north and cover the stars. In no time at all, they would cover the moon, and I wouldn't be able to see my hand in front of my face.

Across the harbor, a light at the back of Henry's house flicked off. Several nights a week I watched Henry's boat round the breakwater on his way to meet with the West Indies trawler that paid him to run drugs into the bay on the Main. Tonight, he'd come back early and shut himself in his house to drink one can of beer after another with his friend Mouse.

I'd always figured that Henry kept his money on his boat, but I'd always been too afraid to row out and check. I'd never considered taking his money—that would be suicide—I just wanted to know where he kept it. The house seemed like too much of a risk. That night I was agitated enough—angry at Henry for having all this money, angry at Danny for taking up everyone's attention, angry at my grandmother and Jacob for paying so much attention to him—that I decided to go take a look. I told myself I would just peek in the foredeck and row back.

Just a few steps down the ladder to the punt, I paused because I felt someone watching me, but no one was there. I gripped the oar handles so hard that my knuckles hurt. You never knew when Henry might step out to smoke a cigarette in his dooryard. Also, a person never knew where Danny would be, day or night. For some reason this made me more determined. I stopped rowing and scanned the edge of the harbor. Dark shags of seaweed lulled against the rocks. No one stirred on the shore trail. My heart pounded in my ears as I muckled the punt to the lee side of Henry's boat and climbed over the gunnel. Henry had a new Cat diesel but never took care of his boat. Paint peeled on the doghouse and the coaming felt spongy. My grandfather'd said Henry would knock the bungs out pounding through the chop and build a new boat for his Cat with his West Indies money. I could barely see by the moonlight as I searched under the foredeck. Nothing there but the precious engine and enough beer cans to fill the smack. He had a new Hydro-Slave even though he never fished, and a live well and bait barrels, all empty.

The shaft for the engine ran under my feet somewhere. Every boat had access. I found a latch, lifted the board, and felt along the side until I found a plastic bag tied to a plank in the bilge. A smart hiding spot. I undid the knot and hauled the bag to the deck. This was it. The money didn't even belong to Henry—that was how I thought. Smuggling money—West Indies money.

I shoved my hand inside the bag and pulled out one of several tightly wrapped packages. When I broke open the plastic, white powder sprayed out and sparked like phosphorescence in the water before dissolving. Dropping the rest on the deck, I looked to Henry's house. No sign that he'd seen anything, not yet. It looked like a bag of flour had exploded at my feet.

Quickly I tried to scoop what had spilled into the bag. It might not belong to Henry at all, was what I thought. Before I could think about what I was doing, I pulled out the other packages, three in all, and ripped them open over the water. I searched under the deck until I found a wrench, stuffed it into the plastic bag, and tossed it overboard. As soon as the bag vanished, I regretted what I'd done.

———

I didn't hate Danny. Once when I was young, he told me, as if it was some kind of secret between us, that fish closed their eyes when it rained. Two winters before the night I found Henry's drugs, I watched Danny shut the door to his shack and nail a board across the doorway from the inside. He didn't come out the next day or the day after. My grandmother had me leave food at his doorstep, which he pulled inside while they slept. I knew it must be hell in that shack. To stay warm, he'd have to turn like a hotdog on a stick in front of the stove. My friend Ames's mother had said Danny was *mental*. Or maybe he wasn't really mental but faking it so he wouldn't have to work like everyone else. I didn't believe, the way many others did, that there was anything seriously wrong with Danny. His thoughts moved sideways like a crab. He always looked to the side as he talked. He couldn't see what was right in front of him, but he noticed things that no one else did. And the rules of life didn't seem to apply to him, not on the island anyway, whereas I was

surrounded by chores, expectations, and dos and don'ts from my
grandmother, who acted more a mother to me than my actual
mother. I'm thankful she did.

One day while I watched his shack through the store window,
I told my grandmother I sometimes thought of Danny as a dog,
which made me like him a bit more.

"You're the one that reminds me of a dog," my grandmother
said. "When I was a girl, we had a black-and-white herd dog.
Used to follow around the cat. So obsessed with that cat that he
hated to blink. When the cat sat, he sat, when the cat walked
across the room, he walked across the room after it. Pretty soon
he forgot he was a dog. Do you understand what I'm saying to
you?"

"No," I said, though I did. I understood perfectly.

It was more than a week before his door flew open and he
stepped out. I was working at the store, watching out the window. I expected someone who'd been cooped up to look at the
sky. The sun was out. When he did glance up, he took a bearing
on a distant spot and marched inland. My grandmother told me
to put on my coat and go see what he was up to. I followed his
footsteps along the road to the middle of the island and past
the church, straight into the woods. It had snowed, rained, and
snowed again. An icy piecrust covered the ground.

When I came out of the woods, I slipped over the ice of Leech
Pond, and there stood Danny in the middle of the pond with
his face raised to the sky. So skinny he could almost fold in half,
he raised one knee then another to his chest as he walked. He'd
taken off his boots. His bony feet lay flat on the ice. His lips were
blistered. "My head is burning," he said. Sweat had stained his
T-shirt.

I ran back to the store for my grandmother, who returned
with my grandfather to fetch Danny off the pond. His fever
didn't break all night. First thing in the morning, we headed for

the doctor on the Main. It was blowing hard and so cold that
spray froze in layers on the deck. My grandfather was afraid we
might turtle. Twice he told my grandmother to take the wheel
while he climbed forward with a hammer to chip away at the ice
on the bow.

———

The morning after I threw Henry's stash overboard, I woke to
find that a front had rolled down and now gusts blew snow into
whirling clouds. Drifts had banked up to the windowsill. Sea
smoke poured off the harbor and spread through the spruce.
Gus's boat was gone; Henry's sat at the mooring. Nothing stirred
behind the windows of Henry's house. I could sense Henry hidden inside, eyelids closed; a clam buried in sand.

My friend Ames rushed into my bedroom and jumped on the
bed with his rubber boots still on.

"Get the boots out of here," I yelled at him. This was our rit-
ual. He knew I hated his damned boots in the bed.

"No, suh!" he yelled back. His voice had deepened prema-
turely, and he sounded like his father. At his house the kids slept
with their boots on because they had no insulation. In the loft
above the kitchen, he woke to the tips of the roof nails covered
in ice.

My grandmother drove us out of the house. We passed drifts
piled high along the edge of the woods. A sudden gust whipped
powder into the sky as we high-stepped together. I felt as if I
were pretending to be my old self, my younger self—the person
I'd been before dumping Henry's drugs into the harbor. A dark
outline appeared on the other side of the field, and I thought it
was Henry, but it was an apple tree.

"I'm gonna be hungry with no breakfast," I complained.

"Want some of my dinner?" Ames pulled a cloth bundle from

his pocket. Biscuits stuffed with nothing, I knew. Ames's family
had been poor forever, for as far back as you could see. Ames
sometimes lived on potatoes and point, we called it—you got a
bowl full of potatoes and pointed to where the meat should be.

I shook my head no to the biscuits—my grandmother would
stop by with my dinner—and I gave Ames the last piece of choc-
olate from my grandmother's supply. Ames snatched the bar
greedily. I couldn't congratulate myself for doing the right thing
because Ames looked stricken.

I opened the schoolhouse door, and there sat Danny at his
regular desk, wearing nothing but socks on his feet, a torn
brown sweatshirt, and the stained canvas trousers my grandmother had given him years before. Skin polished by the cold,
coal-black hair, the longest dark lashes of anyone I'd ever seen.
As soon as Jacob had told him he might be able to go to college if he kept working hard, Danny started showing everyone a
magazine cutout of a red car that would take him all the way to
Miami someday.

Jacob stepped out of the backroom carrying a fresh flannel
shirt, pants, and wool socks that he kept in a trunk, in case, I
suspected, he had to escape my mother. Danny changed and
sat near the stove, but he still smelled like booze, sweat, chum.
Jacob gave Danny his own lunch of biscuits and cheddar and
demanded to know where he'd been hiding, but Danny seemed
not to hear as he tried to use his frozen fingers to shovel food
into his mouth. Everyone in the classroom just watched him
eat. *The prince of stuffing his face,* my mother had once said of
him.

"What're you looking at?" Danny asked me through a mouth-
ful of food.

Even though it'd been just a day, Danny must've thought
enough time had gone by that he could come back and pretend
nothing had happened to all those sheep.

Jacob called for one of the students to fetch more firewood. Only five of us had even come on time this morning. The two who lifted their heads fixed on the blackboard with Pollock eyes.

I volunteered for an excuse to cool the burning skin of my face. I didn't want to feel so angry with Jacob—in my heart I blamed him for what I'd done the previous night. On the way outside, I picked up a piece of split pine from the box so I could knock free the stacked chunks of cordwood. The weather would blow out any time. Snow in late October never stuck for long. The trees at the edge of the field bent in the wind, and a shadow almost twice as large as Ames pushed across the field. It was Henry.

"What?" Jacob asked when I flew open the door. I couldn't speak. Henry banged through after me, lifted Danny out of his seat, and chucked him outside as if he weighed no more than a sack of potatoes. Danny's mouth hung open, he didn't blink, not even when Henry's boot slammed into him. Everyone else spilled out of the schoolhouse, Jacob the last.

"Got your fucking message," Henry yelled at Danny. "Where's it at?" Henry kicked Danny in the head so hard that I felt myself about to throw up. Blood burst from Danny's nose and mouth and sprayed the snow.

"He doesn't know where it is!" I yelled, but no one paid attention to me. Jacob stood there as useless as the Jesus salesman. A gunmetal blue tattoo of a rifle stretched from Henry's wrist to his elbow. His other elbow had a tattoo of a skull. When his teeth clenched, the skull on his forearm twisted. "Open your hole!" Henry said to Danny. When Danny turned away, Henry pried his mouth open and shoved snow inside. Danny spit but Henry scooped up another handful and shoved his fist halfway inside Danny's mouth. I opened my mouth to yell for him to stop, but no sounds came out.

"Up!" Henry said and grabbed Danny by the collar. "You're

gonna show me what you did with it." Henry hauled Danny to
his feet and dragged him across the field. Jacob ran for the trail
that led to my grandparents' house, but there was no time for
that. Racing to catch up with Henry and Danny, I couldn't even
hear the surf over the sound of my own breathing. I ran three
steps to Henry's one, and I still couldn't get ahead of Henry's
tumbling forward. His back was a wall. If Henry shot Danny or
drowned him or gave him to the West Indies people, my grandmother would never forgive me. I wanted Danny off the island,
but not like this.

I called for Henry to stop, but he plowed ahead. I ran faster
and came so close that the snow lifting off the soles of his boots
landed on my thighs. Henry whirled around and leaned forward, his cheeks red. His bottom lip squirmed. Up close his skin
was soft and smooth. *Baby man*, my grandmother called him.

"Go home," he said, then turned and went on. I followed. A
warm patch of his breath hung in the air, smelling of spoiled
milk. As we neared the harbor, the wind switched, the sun cut
through the haze. When we reached the store, Danny broke
free and ran out along the Pinkham's wharf where he fell off the
edge and landed with a crack on the float below. I dogged Henry
to where he lifted his shotgun off a bait barrel.

"You stay there!" Henry commanded, pointing his shotgun at
Danny, who flopped into the harbor like a seal slipping off the
Motion Ledges. Henry headed down the ladder from the wharf
to the float. I followed with my heels almost on his fingers. In
my thoughts, I yelled at Henry the way my grandmother would,
but no sounds would come out of my mouth until I stood on the
float next to him.

"You can take him to Manan, take him anywhere!" I said. I'd
been afraid Henry would kill Danny right in front of me. Now
I wondered if he would kill me, too. Henry stared right past me
as if I hadn't said a word. A shape as long and dark as a blue

shark slipped by in the water. I followed its path to the other side of the dock where the sun caught Danny's eyes and his blue lips rising toward a gap in the planks. His lids closed, his skin tightened over his cheeks, and he breathed out a cloud. His wet clothes would pull him down any second.

Henry ripped out the half-rotten planks where Danny had come up to breathe, but Danny was gone. Another shadow slid under the float, changed directions, and sank into the green. At the stone beach next to the island wharf, Danny's head, then his shoulders, lifted out of the water. When he reached the shallows, he rested on his hands and knees. Steam poured off his back.

That's when I saw Henry raise his shotgun, and I threw my shoulder into his side and sent him flying into the harbor. When Henry came up, I was standing above him. He didn't even know how to dog paddle. I kicked a rope tied to the float in his direction.

Not much happened on the island that people didn't find out about, but no one said a word about what I'd done with Henry's stash. Maybe no one knew. My grandmother kept Danny in her house, locked down for the most part. He seemed happy to stay put. He'd gotten skinny running around in the cold without three meals a day. My grandmother set up a cot by the stove, and when she wasn't there to keep an eye on him, my grandfather and I were supposed to help.

In part because Henry had been rough with me, my grandmother was able to convince Gus to send his son to stay with his wife's people on Manan. Now Gus threatened to come in and get Danny. Said it was for everyone's good, including Danny's, to get him off the island before Henry came back. I'd never seen Gus and my grandmother have such an argument. Maybe this was also why Danny stayed put for as long as he did, a long time for him—maybe two weeks—until we had a concert in the Grange. Dances, people call them, square dances. Old Lem Pinkham usually played the fiddle and people lined up for reels or set up in squares. It was mostly for the kids. Some of the mothers and grandmothers participated. The men smoked in the dooryard, or they sat on the benches set up against the walls and watched, slapping their thighs to the beat. Sometimes at the end of the night when Lem tired, someone put Lynard Skynyrd on the record player and people danced in a kind of free style.

At some point, Sarah showed up. I had no idea she'd returned from Manan. One of her fishermen uncles on her mother's side had dropped her off, and I could see right away that she'd been drinking. Her brother was still on Manan, her father, we knew, was passed out in his fish house, her mother was probably passed out in her bedroom with a cigarette dangling from her fingers. It really was unfair for Gus to blame Danny for Sarah drinking, even if Danny was giving her booze. She had plenty of examples in her own family. I'm sure there was alcohol stashed all over their place. She stumbled around the back of the hall while we danced a reel. It wasn't long before Danny showed up and made a B-line for her. At first, she talked to him, even leaned on his shoulder for a moment, but then she pushed him away. Everyone stopped dancing when she shrieked for him to leave her alone. She stomped out the back door of the Grange leaving Danny standing there with his hands at his sides. Jacob started to approach him, but as soon as he got close, Danny picked up one of the chairs leaning against the wall and smashed it on the floor. He picked up another chair and smashed that one, too. Jacob tried to lay hands on him, but he wriggled free and flew out the door. I was angry that people had stopped dancing—this would be our only entertainment for at least a month. Jacob ran after Danny, and I was left standing there with my grandmother.

The concert ended early. Everyone drifted off home. I was the last one to fall asleep at my grandmother's house and had only been out for a couple hours when I sat up in bed. I knew something was wrong, I just didn't know what. When I came out of my bedroom, I saw the sofa, the woodstove, and the cupboards glowing. It didn't make any sense until I looked out the window and saw fire pouring from the second story windows of Gus's house across the harbor. Flames jumped along the clapboards, pooled in the eaves. I held my hand above the stove, and for a moment the heat from the iron seemed to be the source of what I saw. One of the windowpanes shattered on the second floor of Gus's house. Then my grandmother appeared in her bedroom door, her skin yellow around the dark hole of her mouth. Her right hand floated in the air, her other hand rested on the side of her head. I can still see her in that moment as clearly as if she were standing right in front of me.

"Go wake your grandfather," my grandmother said to me as if she were asking me to toss clam shells into the harbor. I found my grandfather's shoulder and shook him so hard that he grabbed his neck and groaned for me to stop.

"You have to get up!"

"Why do I have to get up?" But his eyes had already fixed on the light growing brighter along the wall. He groped for his socks. "Go!" he told me. "Down to the harbor!" In the kitchen, my grandmother hadn't moved from in front of the window. She told me to find the Indian tanks in back of the store, but the old five-gallon steel tanks we kept for fighting fires had rusted out. Ames and I had tried to use them the previous year to spray each other with water and they hadn't worked.

By the time we reached the store, the fire had whipped up the side of Gus's house. We were all coughing from the smoke. My grandfather and I tugged on the rusted crank siren in front of the store but couldn't make the handle turn. My grandmother had talked about the danger of fire before. Dead spruce, old houses, old wharves, fish shacks, piles of nets and wooden traps, and the shells of old wooden boats. The harbor would burn fast, she'd always said. Flames from lumber and old traps stacked in back of Gus's house jumped through the air. If the wind picked up, the fire would follow the road and maybe hit the Grange. Then up through the middle of the island.

I touched my face and realized snow was falling. My grandmother looked up. The snow was increasing but it could also stop any second. My grandmother got me to help corral the people who were showing up at the harbor. She wanted everyone down at the end of the wharf so we could get them onto boats if necessary. My grandfather and Stoven had gone for their boats. I remember the buttons of my shirt were hot to the touch. I saw the top of a burning spruce next to Gus's house lift, spin into an orange ball, and sail over the water to land on Boynton's boat. Flames started to spread over the doghouse. There was an explosion that sucked the air out of my lungs. One of the rafts in the harbor, where the Boyntons stored fuel. Flames floated in the water. Everyone seemed to move as if they were asleep.

By the time Stoven and my grandfather pulled up to the wharf in their boats, the flurries had turned into a downpour.

"As long as the wind doesn't switch," my grandmother said and then didn't speak as we all watched the rain beat down on the island. The fire in Gus's house continued to burn, but the rain knocked it down some. The wharf didn't burn. As the rain picked up, we all took shelter in the store.

The store smelled of smoke, though not from the woodstove. People huddled under blankets my grandmother kept in the back. Ames and I found some of my grandfather's old clothes and pulled them on even though they were two sizes too big.

I remember seeing Ada huddled with her son Clayton and his son Lawrence. There was also Carl and Tozier and Bennie Coffin and the Hayes's and Big Annie—all people I haven't seen in years—huddled by the stove. My grandmother lit the kerosene lamps and loaded wood into the firebox. I flinched at the sight of the flames. My grandmother, probably colder than all of them combined, still wore her wet clothes.

Each time thick smoke passed the store windows, I felt myself tighten. Maybe the fire would come for us. Maybe we'd have to head for the mainland. Gus swept into the store with his face and arms and naked chest covered in soot. His teeth glowed white. He smelled of smoke and rotten eggs. By now his house had burned down to the foundation.

"They're not here," my grandmother said to him. His belly pushed out and pulled in like the body of a fish laid out on the deck. I turned away as he left. I think some part of me thought the sun would never break again. My grandfather came in. Others did, too. The sound of rain tapping the wharf and voices calling for Flossie and Sarah echoed in the bowl of the harbor. From the other side of the harbor, Gus answered with a seal's moan. Covering my ears to block out Gus, I felt sick to my stomach. If they never found Sarah or Flossie, Gus would only have his son Henry left in the world. Gus pulled out boards. Plunging down again, he scooped up a bundle of sticks, which he lay on the ledge between the house and the water. When he stood, his head arched back, and his hands hung in the air like red claws. Stoven walked out of the woods behind Gus's house with another body. Sarah. I didn't believe it at first. Not yet. Part of her shirt had burned off.

I busied myself popping cans of beans while rain slapped the roof and the fire crackled in the stove. I didn't even really think of Sarah as a Pinkham. She was very pretty, and except for the drinking she wasn't like them at all.

Gus and Stoven carried Flossie to Gus's boat. Sarah lay in Stoven's arms, her salmon-red stomach bent toward the sky, her mouth gulping for air, which meant she breathed. They'd take her to the hospital.

After the rain let up and we had fed everyone and cleaned, I looked at my grandmother. Her face was smudged. She closed her eyes and her cheeks sagged over her jawline. Even Stoven, who worked six to seven days a week, ten hours a day, was tired, with his blackened skin stretched over his cheekbones. When Stoven's mother, Mabel, lost her parents in a storm when she was young, my grandmother's parents took her in and raised her as their own, so Stoven was family to us.

The trees behind Gus's house had turned black. Smoke and steam spread in streams out to sea. In the afternoon my grandmother and Stoven gathered people in the store to talk about what to do. I was worried that they would turn on me. I had assumed that Danny had started the fire because Henry had beaten him up. Henry had beaten him up because he thought Danny had stolen the drugs. It seemed like the others thought Danny had started the fire, too, based on how they avoided looking at my grandmother, who said it had to've been the guys from the trawler, the West Indies boat that supplied Henry with his drugs. Stoven told her the guys on that boat weren't even from the West Indies. They were from New Jersey. He also said that the boat had been over to Manan that night. He'd checked. My grandmother didn't like this at all. She wanted it to be their fault.

"Could've been the stove," my grandmother said and bowed her head, as if she were asking people to feel sorry for her. I wanted her to be right. Stoven said Gus had recently installed a double-walled pipe and done a good job of it, too.

In the morning I saw that soot from the burned bayberry had stained the water of the harbor dark as coffee. Fog drifted through the black trunks. Around noon, I spotted the Coast

Guard Cutter approaching from the west. I figured they'd have the sheriff on board. A Canadian captain had seen the fire and called the Coasties. To Gus, the Coast Guard might as well have been King George's army. No one on the island, including my grandmother, harbored any love for the government. They took your money, told you how to live, snatched your children if you were too poor—in the days before me, they did. Back then, kids hid in trees when the Improvement Society people chased their brothers, sisters, and cousins through the field.

"They'll want to talk to Danny," Stoven said when he caught up to my grandmother. "And you know Gus won't want that. Nothing the state does to Danny is gonna satisfy Gus. They'll set Danny up with free oatmeal." My grandmother didn't want them talking to Danny because anything the state did with Danny would destroy him. We all knew we were going to have to send Danny to the mainland to stay with my grandmother's sister in Appleton.

The Cutter was too deep for the harbor and had to stay on the far side of the breakwater in the swell. They launched one of their rubber boats to carry the sheriff and a few others to the wharf. The sheriff and his men all looked at Gus's burned house with nothing left but the chimney and pieces of wall. The Pinkhams and the Boyntons, up all night like worker ants, had pushed burnt logs and dirt over the rubble.

Jacob showed up from the middle of the island. The Pinkhams, Boyntons, and Cuttings, scarce all morning, lined up. There was Archie Boynton, shifting his eyes over everything and wringing out one arm, then the other. His brother Jimmy had once called my grandmother a fine piece for someone who grew up on war rations. He used to take gambling vacations on the ferry to New Foundland and tell women he was "duty-free."

Others stood around the side of the store in their cut-off sweatshirts over stained long johns. Dressed for fishing today,

like any other day. Except for the Island Meeting in the spring
and concerts at the Grange, and except for the day Danny
drowned all those sheep, we rarely saw this many people from
the island in the same place at the same time. Linda Cutting
and Wishy, standing near each other, hadn't spoken in thirteen
years, since she'd set fire to his truck for reasons unknown.
Most people still living on the island didn't necessarily like each
other; they just hated everyone else.

The Coasties muckled their bowline to a piling, and the sheriff and his men bunched together at the end of the wharf. The
sheriff kicked the blackened boards under his feet and tapped
the badge on his brown jacket. The deputy at his side rested his
hand on his holstered gun. The sheriff and his men had guns
you could see; others on the island had guns you couldn't see.

"Ashes from the stove dumped too close to the house," Stoven
said, as if commenting on the weather, and the sheriff frowned.

"We're going to have to come back with the fire department,"
the sheriff said and raised his eyebrows.

"No reason to bother yourselves," Stoven said.

"I want to know who tried to fill in that cellar hole. Someone
died last night, and I have someone in the hospital," the sheriff
said.

"*We* got someone in the hospital," Stoven said. "None of your
Christly business past the channel nuns." I'd never heard him
refer to himself and the Pinkhams as *we*. He was no friend of the
Pinkhams.

The sheriff told Stoven that things weren't the same as when
Arnold Storey was in the job. We were used to running things
ourselves out on the island. The sheriff rested his hands over his
stomach as if he'd eaten too many beans. Then he yelled over
to Henry asking where his father was. Henry didn't offer up an
answer. Archie Boynton and the Cuttings edged down the hill
toward the wharf. The air buzzed as if lightning had struck the

sea. Henry didn't take his eyes off his feet. The others watched him as carefully as the sheriff, who dragged his toe across the charred boards of the wharf.

"None of you want to know how this happened?" the sheriff said.

"We're fierce on it," Stoven said calmly.

The sheriff aimed his chin at Stoven, seemed to think better of whatever he wanted to say, and waved his guys to follow him to the other side of the harbor. You had to know what to watch for with Henry: eyes down, head drooping, and a wire pulling the muscles between his shoulder blades.

"Do you think I've got time for this?" the sheriff yelled over his shoulder. "For you people out here? I've got work to do."

"I'm not sure you can call it work," Stoven said, as he walked toward the store, "but we'll be happy to see you go back to where they pay you."

Henry and the Boyntons stepped out of the way of the sheriff and the Coasties. At Gus's house, the sheriff leaned over the cellar hole filled with junk. They'd need a backhoe to muck that out, and they wouldn't find anything like that on the island. The sheriff poked around in the dirt with a stick. He'd all the power in the world over us, according to the law, and no power at all on this side of the Minch. The sheriff before this one, Arnold Storey, knew that.

The sheriff and his men stumped back to the wharf and climbed into their rubber boat. Henry boarded his boat and followed them out like some kind of guard dog chasing them out of the dooryard.

My grandmother herded us—Jacob, Stoven, and my grandfather—into the store for cover. It was just starting to rain. Inside, my grandfather started a fire in the stove. That's when Stoven gave us the report on Sarah. She was burned pretty bad. Feet and hands, and she'd swallowed a lot of smoke.

"Listen, Donna," I remember Stoven said, "you know god-damned well this could be the end of it." He wasn't talking about himself. He'd always said if he was going to work for the jeezly ice-cold side of nothing, he'd rather do it out on the island.

We all knew what had to happen. Before the fire, the Pinkhams had been keen to take Danny to the mainland to the state home at Pineland. Now they'd be bent on shipping him—the old punishment. Throw him into a punt with no oars, drag him out, and leave him at sea, as they had the bodies of the sheep Danny had killed.

I went with Jacob to find Danny where he was hiding in one of the old rotting boats pulled up on shore. We both noticed Danny's blackened arms and hands. Jacob asked him if he knew how the fire had started, but Danny wouldn't answer. He only wanted to know about Sarah—where was Sarah? Jacob told him Sarah was at the hospital.

Then he simply said, "I couldn't—" and offered his palm. He stared at the old iron-sick boat where he'd been hiding. Rust from the screws wept over the peeling white paint.

"I want to stay here," he said.

Jacob told him to get moving. We had no time to lose. At the harbor, my grandmother stood next to her door with a bag in her arms. Phil and Stoven waited next to her. Gus had said, "What kind of person would kill all those sheep?" Danny had killed the sheep—made sense that he'd started the fire. My grandfather climbed down the ladder and started the engine. The exhaust boomed. As we headed out of the harbor, my grandmother told Danny that he would remember her sister, even though her sister hadn't been to the island since Danny was five. She said there was money in the backpack. She told him to call her sister from the payphone when he got off the bus. The farm was ten miles from town. Danny had a bag of dimes for the payphone, he had a letter to my grandmother's sister that explained everything. But none of that would matter when he stepped off the bus. He'd been born on the island. No birth certificate, no social security, no license, nothing. The state didn't even know he existed.

We passed the Motion Ledges, where half a dozen black cormorants raised their bills. Danny crouched in the forward cabin, brushed his hair out of his face, and his eyes went from blue to green as he pushed himself into the light. His bony fingers, covered with scars and calluses, gripped a post. Soot stained his face and arms. Jacob had told Danny he could go to college, have his own boat, or that car he wanted.

We sank into a trough and climbed the next peak. A haze had drifted over the sun and the water turned greenish gray. My grandfather's boat, no skiff at thirty-seven feet, bobbed like a cork. The engine muscled the bow up and over each swell. Even though my grandfather had jammed crushed beer cans between the exhaust pipe and the wood roof, the muffler buzzed like a giant insect.

A boat approached fast from the north. It was Henry. My grandfather leaned forward on the throttle, but Henry kept coming at us, wide open. My grandfather ducked his head into the cabin and pulled out a 12-gauge. Henry would have one, too. Henry steered within fifty yards of our starboard side and leaned on his wheel. At the last second, he banked and drenched us with spray. Close to, he yelled that he knew Danny was onboard. My grandfather must've heard him—we all did—but he gave no sign. Henry took his hand off the wheel, aimed his gun forward of my grandfather. Jacob panicked and tried to pull me away and Henry shot into the hull high on the cutwater. My grandfather's face didn't change, but he did pick up his own shotgun. Curling his finger around the trigger, he rested the barrel on the gunnels. Henry stayed parallel to us, close enough to jump from one boat to the other.

"Doesn't matter where you take him," Henry yelled. "I'll find him!"

Henry throttled down, steered broadside behind us, and idled in our wake. As we pulled away, he lifted the shotgun and aimed the barrel at the back of my grandfather's head. I held my breath and thought I would leap between my grandfather and Henry, but I didn't, and Henry lowered his gun and swung his bow in the direction of the island.

My grandfather tossed his gun back into the cabin. "Don't have any goddamned shells on board," he said. My grandmother had said that Gus and Henry were tyrants of their own patch and would not risk anything on the mainland. I wasn't so sure.

At the wharf in Dennis, a bunch of guys wearing sweatshirts razored off at the shoulders and dirty rubber Grundens pretended not to check us out. They'd've heard about the fire and be thinking about the grounds around the island. Most of the Dennis fishermen didn't have big enough boats to fish out that far, but they knew people in Jonesport and Manan where a lot of guys had larger boats. My grandfather had called them seagulls waiting to feed off other people's misfortune.

We walked up the cracked street past the stores. Wilson's, Percy's. The customers in the Dennis Diner turned to face the window. The teller in the bank watched us. Eyeing the bricks in front of his feet, Danny seemed to have crawled inside himself. My grandmother took his arm as she had many times before. She reminded him to call from the payphone when he got to Camden. Told him everything would be fine, which was just as much a lie as telling him he could have whatever he wanted.

We were handing out a lesser punishment, and not only for Danny's sake. Danny was paying for all of us. He was paying for me. He would travel through hills he'd never seen to sleep under a strange sky in Appleton. My grandmother spoke to Danny as if he were a child, and he nodded, lowering his head at what she said. The whole island had treated Danny as a child, but now we were sending him away where the world would treat him as an adult.

The bus arrived. The driver hopped down the steps, scooped up Danny's bag, and pitched it into the cargo hold with the rest of the luggage. My grandmother gave the man money for the ticket and told him where Danny should get off. The driver shrugged. Except for the few times a year he came to Dennis, Danny never saw strangers.

Jacob hugged Danny while Danny stood there with his arms at his sides waiting for it to be over. He boarded without turning around and took the first empty seat around the corner from the door. My grandmother tapped on the window and waved, but he only stared straight ahead.

I tried to imagine him watching the forests on both sides of the road. I knew the route from having visited my great aunt: Machias, Columbia Falls, Milbridge, Stueben, Gouldsboro, Ellsworth, Orland, Bucksport, Belfast, Searsmont, if the bus even turned off Route 1. Most of the towns would have a brick Main Street almost identical to the Main Street in Dennis, surrounded by white colonials and fishermen's cottages like those in Dennis and the island. Danny would notice the small differences, though, the names on the store windows all wrong, the houses positioned at funny angles to the road, the people coming out of the post office dressed in familiar clothes but wearing strange faces.

A couple days after we dropped Danny off at the bus stop, I was sitting on the breakwater with my transistor radio. School was canceled for the day, maybe for the whole week, because of the fire. Sometimes, on a clear day, I could capture Howard

Cosell's *Wild World of Sports* on the radio. Not today. I found a song that sounded like one of my grandfather's records without the scratchiness, and I turned up the volume as a white triangle slid across the horizon. A large yacht headed south with its sail bellied. Every fall they chased the warm winds all the way to the West Indies, my grandfather said. Boats loaded with nothing but the people who sailed them.

The season had arrived for lengthening the warps into deep water, so all the men were out except my grandfather. The barometer had fallen—I could feel the dip in the back of my throat—and a shiny glin appeared on the sea to the north. The weather would turn that night.

My grandfather waved to me from his wharf. He wanted my help hauling traps, which had been soaking long enough to starve the lobsters inside. Underway, I leaned over the side to check on the buckshot pellets from Henry's shotgun buried in the cutwater, high on the bow. My grandfather said the boat knew its own muscle; he'd bung the small holes and repaint the hull in the spring.

Outside the harbor, he gunned the engine. It was ebb tide with high rollers. The rail shook, and we rose over the top of a swell into the sky. At the top of the next swell, I felt as if I were standing in the bell tower of the chapel and looking over the island and the sea for miles.

I found myself wondering if Danny felt alone. At the same time, I wanted to know how much money my grandmother had put in his backpack. We couldn't afford to give money away to Danny. I almost had a hole in the bottom of my rubber boot. No matter what, though, I thought Danny had gone to Appleton; we could go back to the way things were. But I also felt I had to be careful not to jinx it. I promised myself I would listen at church when the *Sunbeam* arrived with the minister for his winter Jesus visit, I'd never disobey, never talk back to my mother.

School would begin. Sarah would return soon, and we were about to start on geometry, which would help me get ready for surveying. Jacob and I could talk again about my training to work as an assistant.

For the first time, I looked forward to the dead of winter, even for the February volleyball game that never usually counted as fun: an old fishing net stretched across the dance floor; a bunch of people in rubber hip boots smacking a half-dead basketball with one hand while they drank beer with the other hand and bobbed to the Rolling Stones. Most evenings my grandfather and I would play cribbage by the stove that would tick and glow against the drafts.

We approached my grandfather's grounds off the Motions and started what would be hours of looping around the buoys. I reached over with the gaff to hook the line. He ran the slack through the Hydro-Slave under the fairlead and hit the brass handle on the dash that controlled the hauler. The line spun taught and coiled itself on the deck. I tossed the buoy on the gunwale next to the house. The line strained with the weight of the pots being pulled from the bottom; the rope popped as it pinched between the plates.

I worked fast to square the pot on the gunnel, flip open the door to the kitchen, and begin to toss the shorts back into the ocean. Sometimes I wished I were the son of one of the real lobstermen on the island. By dint of hard driving, they knew things I didn't. By nine they could winterize an outboard, caulk a sheer strake, bend spruce boughs. They knew how to swell planks, how to read a high glassy swell or the panicked terns flying low, seine for poggies, one hundred poggies to a gallon of oil worth three dollars. I knew how far to lengthen out as the air turned heavy. Sort the mail, run the cash register, keep the accounts. I could run the store. Girl's work, was what the other boys called that behind my back.

My grandfather slowed the hauler down as the first pot on the next string broke the surface and rose beside me. I opened the bag, shook what was left of the old bait into the water as gulls circled overhead, grabbed a bag of fresh herring from a bucket, and fixed the bag onto the cleat inside the trap. Two lobsters snapped in the kitchen. They looked like shorts. One breeder.

We worked in silence except for the voices that sometimes chirped on the radio above the sound of the engine. Late in the afternoon, he turned off the Hydro-Slave with the last string jammed in the plates, shut off the engine, and sat on the gunwale facing the island in the distance. The line held against the current as I pulled out the bag with cheddar sandwiches my grandmother had made for us that morning. My grandfather held his in his lap and closed his eyes. The cold salt air, heavier here than on the island, filled my lungs. It felt as if I hadn't taken a deep breath in weeks. My grandfather lit his pipe instead of eating, and my nose stung with the smoke.

"This summer, you and me'll drive to Bangor for some of that good cheddar," he said. "We'll have to come up with some excuse for your grandmother."

Every summer, my grandfather and I drove to Bangor to the marine store, and on the way, we stopped for the best cheddar at a place called Ingersoll's. When we crossed the bridge and dipped down the hill into the old downtown, I would lean forward to see the sagging wires draped over wooden poles. Fat gray birds the size of fists would sit in groups on the wire, staring down. It was an unusual sight for me, then.

My grandfather would buy two slices of cheddar, one for me and one for himself, and two bottles of Coke, and we would eat in silence under a giant oak tree. We didn't have many hardwood trees on the island. Away from the sea, the air would warm. On the way back to Dennis in the truck, my thighs would stick to the vinyl seats. The fields would be open on both sides of the road. Forests and fields and roads and cities like Bangor spread as far across the land as the ocean was wide. It was hard to imagine.

"We'll let this last one soak," my grandfather said. His fingers stayed bent after the line fell into the water. I knew we should move all the strings—we had no more than a dozen keepers to show for our work—but I didn't want to say anything. I'd never seen him so tired.

"I never thought Danny would do something like start the fire," I said.

My grandfather raised his eyebrows.

"I don't hate him," I said. "I never wanted any of this to happen." I wanted to say more but was afraid to.

"Of course, you didn't."

I asked if he thought Danny would be happy with Grandma's sister.

"Anyway," he said as he nudged the throttle with the heel of his hand, "I think your grandmother's cooking *scud missile* tonight to punish us for the work we ain't even failed to do yet."

Scud missile was my grandfather's name for the leftovers my grandmother dumped into a tin and baked in the oven.

"She's been feeding the whole island since the fire," my grandfather said, "so now every supper's gonna be a kick in the ass."

As we motored slowly toward the island, I watched the black trail of our exhaust drift into the sky. The white houses surrounding the harbor on the island glowed in the light. We arrived at dusk, unloaded the catch into the co-op pound, and headed for the wharf. My grandfather said we would clean the boat in the morning. It was not like him to put it off. I cleated the painter, and we rowed to the wharf. In the store, my grandmother gave my grandfather the eye only briefly when he took four Mary Anne's—two for me, two for him—from my grandmother's stash.

We drank our tea and ate the cookies. I felt the familiar drowsiness from the heat of the stove. The light began to dim, and Stoven appeared on the harbor trail stumping toward us. It was a comfort to see him headed to the store at the end of the day. Nothing could be more natural. He opened the door with a lot of care not to rattle the bell. It seemed to take him a long time to cross the room and even longer for him to drag a stool closer to the stove. He stood above the stool and breathed unevenly.

"Sarah's dead," he said. His job done, he sat on the stool. My grandmother's face hardened, and I felt a numbness pass through my body and thoughts. Stoven, who'd cut and bandaged his thumb earlier that day, rested his wounded hand on his lap. I thought of Sarah's hand dangling in the air as Stoven carried her to the boat. No one bothered to light one of the lamps, so we sat in darkness. My grandmother opened the stove door and dropped another log on the burning coals.

In the morning, I walked with my grandfather to his trap lot on a rise behind the house and sat on a stump overlooking the windless harbor. Streaks of black ash ran to the water's edge. None of the boats had left that morning. In my grandfather's trap lot, bundles of buoys and toggles hung like apples from branches above piles of coiled 20- and 30-fathom pieces of line. Two old barrels full of garbage sat next to the remains of a shack. My grandfather's unshaven jaw hung loosely. Even though he held his ax in his lap, he seemed as if he'd decided there was no point in doing any kind of work. I wondered if maybe everyone on the island had decided the same thing. No fishing, no school, no store. I stood upright, but I felt myself hurling forward at the same time.

My grandfather said we should go down to the store and have some tea. His knees cracked as he stood, and midway down the slope, he stopped and looked over the breakwater to the Minch. A boat appeared on the range. Maybe the West Indies trawler, I thought at first, but no—a Manan fishing boat. Not a strange sight. I'd almost turned away when I spotted a smaller boat towed behind the larger one. The boats approached as my grandfather and I watched. After a while, the Manan boat separated and headed northeast while the smaller boat rose to the peak of a swell and sank in the trough.

"What is that?" my grandfather asked. I didn't answer. What we saw made no sense: the boat, seventeen feet or so, a dory with a high bow and stern, had two long sticks on either side— oars lifting as the rower leaned forward over his knees. Half a dozen of these dories floated in our harbor. My grandfather owned one himself, but a person couldn't row across the Minch in one, even towed partway. The boat disappeared in the trough of another swell and appeared again a moment later.

My grandfather told me to go fetch my grandmother, and I took off toward the store. My grandmother grabbed the edge of the counter. I yelled that he was back, and she was out the door and onto the wharf. Danny rounded the breakwater and entered the harbor with his back swaying in slow motion. I checked over my shoulder to see if anyone else had seen. By the time the dory nudged the wharf, Danny seemed about to fall over. The engine well held an old outdrive; gas cans covered the floor. Danny twisted his head around and squinted at us. My grandmother didn't speak for what felt like a long time. Then she said Danny's name, which seemed to give him permission to climb the ladder. His palms were bleeding from pulling on the oars. He climbed using his wrists as hooks over the rungs. When he stumbled onto the wharf, my grandmother said, "Why're you here?" Not the voice she used on my mother, with words that felt like a wall. Not the way she talked to my grandfather, in short little nips. The same voice she used with me.

Danny pointed his blistered hand west. "I couldn't see the water anymore. I told the driver to stop the bus," he said. I believed him. "One of the Manan boats towed me across the Minch." He rubbed his face with the back of his hand. Blood smeared across his cheek. He had deep circles under his eyes and looked as if he hadn't slept since he boarded the bus. "Dropped me off so I could see the island." The skin of his neck was red from the sun. Then he asked where Sarah was. The rest of us were quiet. When my grandmother told him, Danny blinked, took two steps, and collapsed to his knees.

My grandmother and I helped Danny up to the house where she had her medical kit. She helped him pull on a pair of my grandfather's boots and wrapped gauze around his fingers. Then I saw Henry across the harbor standing in his dooryard carrying his shotgun. He seemed to hear the distant sounds of a diesel engine at the same time I did. Out in the Minch, a boat plowed toward the island. Gus coming back from the hospital. The people he knew on Manan would've told him by radio that Danny was heading to the island.

My grandmother barked at my grandfather, who went for his gun. He took his time checking the breach and finding the shells in the closet. My grandmother shoved Danny into the bedroom and closed the door as Henry banged into the kitchen. His eyes, passing over each one of us, jumped in his head. He thumbed the stock of his gun but kept the barrel pointed at the floor. My grandfather inserted the second shell into the barrel and closed the breach. He also kept the barrel pointed at the floor.

The air tasted of metal. Henry's face sucked up all the light. A balloon rose in my chest as he crashed around the kitchen, knocking a pot onto the floor. He leaned into my grandmother's bedroom as if he owned the place. The way he stepped declared that he owned all of us. At last, he turned the knob on my bedroom door. Locked. He punched the door open with his hip and stepped inside. His tongue curled over his bottom lip. The window was raised, Danny was gone.

Henry took his time scanning the woods behind the house. When he turned, his eyes skipped over me as if I wasn't there, and he stumbled down the trail to his father's house. Gus plowed toward the harbor and in a few minutes pulled up to his wharf.

I knew Danny had headed to the school where the heavy shutters bolted from the inside and the storm door could be locked. My grandmother stood on the stoop. My grandfather leaned over the table with the shotgun in his hand. We just waited. It took about an hour for the Pinkhams to return with Danny and load him into Gus's boat. They tied a punt off the stern and headed east out of the harbor.

Several weeks later, the Pinkhams left for the mainland for good. The Boyntons, who had lost their boat in the fire, left before the Pinkhams—they were the first to go. Several other families left, and that was it. Without their money, we couldn't maintain the store. My grandmother's debt to Percy's in Dennis outweighed what she could hope to collect. If people paid what they owed her, we might've been able to make it a bit longer. But the people who owed the most could least afford to pay. The goddamned Boyntons and Cuttings owed so much money on their gear to the dealer in Dennis that my grandmother would have to get in line. By the time I could really understand what was happening, we'd spent two weeks sharing rooms at a cheap motel in Bangor that Jacob had paid for with his savings.

"Some of the other guys are talking about selling their rigs to get out from under it," Stoven said when he came to see us at the hotel. He spoke to the wall instead of looking any of us in the eye. My grandmother put her hand on his arm. She didn't want to hear any more.

"Carl's got his ticket in electric," Stoven said. "He can work anywhere."

"So do you," my grandmother said, and that's when Stoven told us he planned to head for Sheet Harbor in Nova Scotia where he'd cousins. He could sell his boat and start over. I didn't blame him, but the news was more than my grandmother could bear.

Stoven also had news from the sheriff's office, where he knew people. They'd found gas cans in Gus's house, but they were not used to start the fire. Just empty chainsaw cans already in the house. So, there was no telling who had started the fire. The fire department had gone out there and pulled apart the wreckage as well as they could. They thought the fire had started on the second floor in the main bedroom. The room where Gus's wife, Flossie, who often drank and smoked in bed, had been sleeping on the night of the fire.

My mother came to see us at the hotel, hugged me, barely spoke to Jacob, and immediately headed out for a new job in Nova Scotia with someone Stoven knew. My grandfather lined up a short-term job three hours south, here at the Iron Works in Carleton. They could use someone who had worked as a harbor pilot. The job would start soon, and we had to get down there. Jacob found us an apartment walking distance from the plant, the school, and the grocery store. Two bedrooms for the unbelievable sum at the time of three hundred dollars. I didn't know what we'd do when my grandfather's temporary job ran out.

The temperature had fallen on the day we arrived in Carleton. We crossed high on the Carleton Bridge, and I could see the jagged line of buildings along the river and the peaked roofs of houses spreading up the hill. More than ten times the size of

Dennis, and with the constant traffic of Route 1 flowing over the bridge—I wondered how we would live there.

For weeks, shadows ringed Jacob's eyes. When he woke in the morning, he seemed more tired than when he'd gone to bed. One morning, he said he wanted to show me what he'd discovered while driving around when we were staying in the hotel. My grandmother and my grandfather had walked to Front Street, so I followed Jacob to the truck parked in front of the apartment. We headed toward the edge of town. On the riverbank, the Iron Works rose as large as a city, with cranes and steel buildings and two large gray warships. I'd never seen anything like it.

I rolled the window open an inch because the cab smelled like sweat, rotten fish, and gravy poutines, like every other truck I'd been in. We passed long stretches of trees, a gas station, a hardware store, a lumberyard, more trees, heading east at first, though after a while I didn't know. If I kept quiet, if I sat still, maybe we'd drive to Dennis and take my grandfather's boat to the island. Maybe Jacob'd come with me. I focused on the trees and tried not to see the buildings and cars and telephone poles and the way in which the land opened to stretches of marsh.

"Over the last couple weeks, I've been borrowing your grand-father's truck," Jacob said. "A waste of gas, I know, but I had to get out, and I wanted to show you this place I found."

We turned onto a narrow road that rose up a hill. High above, white clouds pulled apart. We passed into woods filled with the same kind of trees I'd always known.

Eventually Jacob turned onto a rutted drive, no wider than the truck. The front wheels leaned into the hill, tires spitting gravel, springs groaning. He gunned the engine, and we came into the open on level ground: an old field clean of stones where two tire tracks vanished into knee-high grass that grew into shadows. Except for my mother's house and the sound of Boom Beach, this could've been Tarr's Field.

"She'll come back, my mother," I said. I knew Jacob often pictured my mother in Tarr's Field, and that he probably suspected the truth that he'd lost her forever.

Jacob slid out of the truck and, wandering into the field with the fingers of his right hand brushing the grass, he rested his other hand on top of his head, as if afraid he might lift off the ground like a balloon.

"It's five acres," he said, turning toward me and waving his hand toward the field sweeping to the tree-line. "Down there below us: all state land, and on these other three sides, state land. No one can build around us," he said. His lower lip drooped, his eyes squeezed shut. He didn't seem happy at all, and behind him, the land looked empty, the islands in the bay unmoored.

"I'm going back to the island," I said. The words came out of my mouth before I knew what I was saying. For a moment I thought Jacob hadn't heard me.

"There's nothing there," Jacob said. "I mean there will only be a few still living there."

He said my name like he was calling on someone in class. Someone he didn't know very well.

"Even Stoven is leaving," Jacob went on. "And Henry and Gus are using the harbor to stage from, I heard, but they moved the family to Dennis. The Cuttings might be there part-time. Their families moved to the mainland, though. I think maybe Vince is there. This is all from your grandmother. Some guy from Portland wants to buy up land to sell for cottages." He opened his mouth to say more but then remained quiet.

I'd never thought that someone else might own my grandparents' land or house or my mother's house. Over the years, I'd heard about Gus and Lem Pinkham buying up pieces of land on the island from people who needed money to get through winter, but people talked as if the Pinkhams were doing them a favor. As soon as the fishing improved and people had money again, they'd buy the land back. I'd never thought of the house where my mother lived as even belonging to my mother. My grandmother had grown up there with her grandmother. Someday I would run the store.

"My mother can't give the house away."

"Not give it away. They're going to have to sell," Jacob said, but I couldn't make sense of the words. I wondered about the kids from school.

The field where we stood didn't seem right. More dirt than salt. I shaded my eyes to get a clear view of the distant ocean and the small islands that marked the entrance to the bay. The people who lived out there, on those islands, must have schools and stores and fields and kids as old as me.

"I killed Danny," I told him, and of course that was why all this was happening.

Jacob's jaw clenched. The skin above his cheekbones screwed up—a look I'd only seen once, directed at my mother.

"No," he said. "Why would you say that?"

"I told Gus about seeing him and Sarah together. I don't even know what I saw anymore. Then Gus sent Sarah to Manan, then…."

Jacob shook his head. "No," he said.

I couldn't bear to mention the bag I'd taken from Henry's boat and emptied into the harbor. I would never tell anyone— certainly not my mother, not even a stranger—what I'd done that night. I'd wanted Danny out of the way, and I'd wanted to travel with Jacob. My mother would say, "See, Corson, you got what you wanted." One of her favorite sayings.

Now I've said more than I meant to say.

Jacob held so still I wondered if he felt ill. "Things won't be like this forever," he said after a few minutes. I waited for him to say what we would do. He always had a plan.

"There's an old cellar hole over there." Jacob pointed to his right, his eyes following the curve of the land. "If I made some money out West, and we sold the property on the island, maybe we could build toward the back of the field. I'd put a barn right next to the house," he said. "A house, two stories, dormers on top facing the field. We'll have to get power here, of course, that's the first thing, and we'll have someone else do the foundation. Drill a well. We could all live here—your grandparents, you. Maybe your mother would come back. Not for me, but you'd have both of us. I could find a job around here, your mother could, too, and you could go to school, which is only five miles down the main road."

Jacob told me more about the house in his head: two rooms upstairs under the eaves, woodstove in the kitchen, pine floors, an old cast-iron tub—the house I'd grown up in, my mother's house. I stopped hearing what Jacob said and watched his face: the color rising in his cheeks as he pointed to where the barn would sit. I could see myself walking through the field that looked over the bay.

"Will you at least think about living here and talk to your grandparents about the idea?" he said. We climbed into the truck and drove carefully downhill to the main road. When we reached the tar, he asked again if I'd really think about the plan. I said yes, but this land Jacob wanted, an island in the sky, seemed less and less real the faster we drove.

"I have to go on a job out in Alberta," Jacob said, "or we'll never have the money to do this," he said. Now he seemed as far away as the time before he came back to the island.

I'd always thought of myself as someone prepared for any kind of trouble, someone who would never panic in the worst situation, and here I struggled to think clearly. I couldn't picture what would happen, not even in the next few minutes. I thought of Henry and Gus loading Danny into Gus's boat and heading for the outside with a punt in tow. The old one with rust weeping over the white paint. Miles out to sea, they would've set him in the punt with no motor, no oars. Nothing but his bare arms. Danny might've survived the first day, as the current took him north toward the Grand Banks, but by the end of the second day, the wind would've pushed the waves as high as steeples.

———

We dropped Jacob off at the bus stop. From there he went to the airport and out west to a job. He said he'd be back in six weeks. He marked it on a calendar that he left in my bedroom. My grandmother asked how I was feeling that evening, and I said I was "okay." Same thing I said every time she asked. I knew she was asking how I felt about Jacob leaving, but I didn't want to discuss it.

One morning I listened to my grandmother wrestle with the faucet on the shower. Jacob had explained how to use the thing, and I had shown her half a dozen times by now. My grandmother grumbled and called for my grandfather. Busy dressing for work in the bedroom, he pretended not to hear. My grandmother might never figure the faucet out for herself.

"I have to go to work," my grandfather said.

I said I would go with him and walk back on my own. Down High Street to North, down North to Washington, and south by the row houses to the shops, I said nothing to my grandfather and he said nothing back. We both knew my grandmother didn't like the idea of me walking back across this town alone. We passed under the towering iron and concrete bridge, where cars growled over the metal grating.

"You better hurry home before your grandmother gets out of the bath," my grandfather said.

"Nothing will happen," I said, "I can find my way." I'd

memorized the streets. But as we approached the three-story metal wall that surrounded the Iron Works and extended along the riverbank, I couldn't be so sure where I was. No windows, no doors, no vents. Several large cranes loomed above. A guarded chain-link area marked the entrance. It's the same now, more or less. A man in front of us wearing a white helmet and carrying a metal lunchbox showed an ID card, passed a checkpoint, and ducked through a doorway in the wall.

"What do you do in there?" I asked, not for the first time.

"I show people how to make things that float."

"What *really*?" I said.

"I tell them they've been doing everything all wrong, building cruisers with the bridge too high off the deck."

I didn't want my grandfather to work on the other side of the wall even for a day. I knew he had no choice, so I kept my mouth shut. When we reached the checkpoint, he sighed.

"You go right home," he said and took out the plastic card with his photo and name next to the letters CIW. His eyes, black at the centers, had grayed around the edges. He blinked at me. I thought I could hear a low hum, pistons and gears maybe, coming from behind the fortress walls. A great engine grinding away. Metal levers and wheels turning. Burning oil.

"I'll be back in eight hours. Nothing's going to happen to me, you'll see. I go in, I come out, they give me money. It's easy—easiest thing in the world," he said, but I'd already seen his hands curled in his lap at the end of the day, and his eyes closed above lined cheeks. Every day he entered that building seemed to slow him down. He showed the guard his ID and stepped carefully, as if afraid he might slip, down the walkway. He didn't glance over his shoulder when he opened the door and passed to the other side of the steel wall. The door stood ajar for a moment and slammed shut.

Jacob had been gone for more than two weeks when I decided
to take a walk on my own one night. I couldn't wait any longer.
I took the money I'd earned from working in the store and hidden in one of the logbooks, stuffed two changes of clothes into
a bag with a loaf of bread, and I slipped out of the apartment
hours before dawn.

I planned to take the bus to Dennis. From there I'd find one of
the Pinkhams headed out to the island and ask for a ride across
the Minch. The store would be there on the island, and my
grandmother's house would be there—I couldn't really believe
they would be for sale.

As I walked down Washington Street, my heels struck faster.
My grandmother and my grandfather didn't understand yet, but
they couldn't live here in this town, where people didn't sound
right, and nothing looked right to us. Most people in Carleton—
they wouldn't have understood. The island where I had lived,
where my family had lived since the early 1700s, wasn't just a
place to live. I sat on the bench next to the bus stop across from
Gediman's Appliance Store. From several blocks away, I could
hear the traffic on Route 1 crossing the Carleton Bridge. Other
noises—trucks rumbling in the distance and dull thudding,
maybe from the Iron Works—filled the air. There was a chance
that when Jacob finished with his work in Alberta, he would
never come back.

I heard the high growl of the engine before I spotted the
round headlights. The bus pulled to a stop and the light from
the streetlamp reflected my face in the corrugated silver door:
long across the brow, compressed around the mouth, eyes on
one of the metal seams. The door rumbled open, and the driver
raised his eyebrows. The gray skin under his chin rolled into his

neck. The bus could take me to Dennis, and from there maybe I could get a ride out to the island.

"Are you getting on?" he asked, and for some reason the long, throaty groan of the *on* made my legs freeze. If Jacob were there, he'd ask what I planned to burn for firewood when we got to the island. My grandfather hadn't gotten his wood in yet. We had enough for a month. Also, Jacob'd want to know how we'd make money or even feed ourselves once the food in the store ran out. With no school, nothing to sell in the store, what was there? We didn't know much about fishing—just what I knew from hauling a few traps outside the harbor with my grandfather. I hated shrimp but liked clams—my second favorite food after hot dogs. I dug every year with my grandfather, who'd taught me to put the hoe on over them, roll them, without busting the shells. Clams were good to eat, with other things, but a person couldn't clam for a living. That's what you did before you starved.

The bus driver's impatience boiled into his lips.

"No, you're not going?" he said.

He closed the door. Long after the sound of the engine vanished, diesel fumes hung in the air around me. No one else on the street, no lights shone in the storefronts. It started to rain and soak through to my scalp. I tilted my head and watched the drops arc through the air in the glow of the streetlamps.

Not wanting anyone to stop and ask me what I was doing, I stood and walked toward the onramp for the Carleton Bridge. It was a day's drive to Dennis—I couldn't walk there—but I couldn't go back to the apartment. I didn't know where I was going. The rain stung my cheeks as the wind increased, and halfway across the river on the bridge, I stopped. To my right, the Iron Works rose on the banks. The people there worked in 8-hour shifts 24 hours a day. Some of them seemed to crawl like ants over the deck of a military boat. When I turned away to face the wind and the rain, the afterimage of the lights burned in my vision. The sound of the river flowing around the pilings below seemed to fill the air around me. Muddy water full of rotting trees and fish and worse, all pushed under my feet.

My grandfather had heard at work that a lobster boat had turned over in the chop where the current ripped into the sea, a few miles downriver. Two years seemed like a lifetime ago, and I strained to picture exactly what Jacob's father, Everett, looked like as he rowed out to the harbor and threw himself over the side: bald, blue eyes, only half his front teeth, deep lines down his cheeks. Maybe, though, his eyes had been gray green to match the harbor. His arms might've been short. I couldn't remember if he wore a dirty T-shirt or a torn plaid shirt. I kept rethinking the picture. As soon as I thought I could see him, he'd change. I went with my grandfather in the boat to drag the bottom. My grandfather's pipe spewed smoke in front of his face, but I could still see his eyes flashing like herring turning against the race. Once we reached Everett's boat, my grandfather tossed the grappling hook, and we snagged almost right away. My grandfather slung the line through the Hydro-Slave, and Everett came over with his eyes open wide.

I rested my hands on the railing, the metal cold as seawater. I could climb over and never have to see this place again. The current would take me to the mouth of the river and push me out to where Danny was, where I deserved to be.

The sky had begun to lighten. Where the current ripped, the river folded into itself. I pictured my grandmother standing in the apartment with her palm pressed to the window glass as she searched up and down the street for any sign of me.

Almost too stiff and hungry to move, I trudged back the way I'd come. My teeth hurt from grinding. I checked my grandfather's watch and discovered the hands had stopped. A block away, I saw the fore door of the apartment open, letting in the cold. I almost tripped as I ran up the steps. My grandmother, not at the window, sat with her face in her hands. My grandfather stood with his back to the door. His hair was soaking wet—he'd been out searching for me in the rain. When my grandmother raised her head, I didn't recognize her. Dark stains pooled under her eyes, her mouth hung as if from rubber bands, her hair stuck to her forehead, and her chapped lips trembled. My grandfather quickly shut the door. Only then did she eyeball me from top to bottom and sigh. In another time, she would've been on her feet already, pushing me toward the stove and pulling off my wet clothes.

"Go on, then," my grandfather whispered. "Get changed." I took some fresh clothes out of the trunk. From the bathroom, I could hear my grandfather put on the new kettle, take bread out of the cupboard, jam from the shelf. I changed as quickly as I could and returned to the front room. My grandmother didn't raise her eyes. I'd been foolish to think I would take the bus back to Dennis. Jacob—and even sometimes my mother—acted as if they were alone in the world. Just because everyone else had left my grandparents didn't mean I could. I didn't have that choice, and I would never make the mistake of thinking so again.

———

It was a week or so after I had tried to take the bus back to Dennis. It must've been early in the morning. I remember freezing rain pelting the window. I woke feeling as if the floor rocked with swells and opened the closet door so I could put on my boots. I'd never had a closet before—a room within a room. In addition to my boots, I found the white and blue sneakers I'd worn to the concert on the island and hadn't seen since. I lifted one of the sneakers and ran my finger along the inside of the sole. Not my sneakers but an exact copy. My grandmother's doing.

Ringing from the parlor made me jump. It could be my mother, I thought, calling to say she wasn't coming back after all. Or it could be Jacob calling. In the dark, I followed the wall with my hands, pushing my stocking feet along the floors until I reached the kitchen and the phone Jacob had installed. My mother would have a list of excuses for why she wasn't coming back right away. Jacob would want to hear the NOAA report on the visibility between the Isle of Shoals and Roque Island. Maybe he didn't quite believe, as I didn't, that we'd left the island. Suddenly the thing shut up. I lifted the receiver—a static buzz filled my ear.

"You didn't get it in time," my grandmother said from the doorway to her bedroom. Not angry, just a statement. My grandmother stared at the phone as if it were a dog that might bark any moment. She'd lost weight; her coat draped off her shoulders like a board cloth off a table.

We didn't need to be awake. No school, no store. Every morning we rose early and dressed for nothing. Sleet scraped the windows. My grandmother said, "Sit," and the sound of her voice, so familiar, brought me back to the room. When she fussed at the stove, I noticed a letter open on the kitchen table. My grandmother never did anything by accident. The envelope had no return address, but I recognized Stoven's handwriting from the notes he'd sometimes left in the store. *Batteries, soap, penny nails.* Things he needed from Percy's on the Main. Stoven left an address with no postal code at the bottom of the page. The letter read like a ship's log. *Boyntons to Harrington. Gilleys to Sullivan Harbor where Elizabeth's parents live. Vince Cuttings to Jonesport. Daryl to Machias where he bought a piece of land years ago. Gotts, Hayes's, Coffins, and Tarboxes to Dennis. Henry and Gus and that lot to Dennis and to fish the island from the Main. Grover I don't know. I am to Sheet Harbor.*

Just as Jacob had said, everyone was gone. By the time my

grandmother turned back from the stove and saw the letter in my hands, light had filled the kitchen. I looked through the window, and I remember I couldn't tell the difference between the rippled glass and the channel of rainwater flowing down the street.

"Your grandfather already left for the Iron Works," my grandmother said. "The early shift."

She set the teapot on the table, and I returned the letter to the spot where I'd found it. I wished other letters would come— from Jacob, my mother. Anyone. I thought of Robbie and Hannah and Mary and Cora and Lenora and Albert, but especially my friend Ames, probably living in some steam box of a room with his parents. They had people in Machias. I hadn't even spoken to Ames since I'd left the island. I'd started a letter to him, but my grandmother didn't have an address yet.

My grandmother believed I needed to keep moving—we had to walk every morning. I wanted to stay in the kitchen where I could sit at the table and rest my feet on one of my trunks, but she took our coats off the hook and told me to hurry before the weather turned again.

We stepped onto the front landing. The rain had let up. No salt in the air, only the must and damp of a root cellar, and I couldn't feel the crashing surf in my knees. We're just upriver from the ocean here in Carleton, but for someone like me it was as if we had moved to another country.

We followed the usual route past the store windows on Front Street. One sold dresses, another men's coats and hats, another vacuum cleaners and hardware. We had no use for any of it— that's what I thought at the time. We passed a Wilson's Drugs just like the one in Dennis and turned up Washington Street where lights shone in the houses. Across from the Patten Free Library, where I would spend more than half my life working with Janet, I looked over my shoulder and saw the stone clock tower on the bank building and church spires spaced between the white and black chimneys of old houses. At this point, my grandmother and I normally headed back to the apartment, but she wanted to walk farther up the street.

"We'll go a little more every day," she said.

I heard car wheels crunching over road sand behind us. We stopped and watched one car and three more pass, trailing a cloud of exhaust. Halfway up the hill, another car went by, and somewhere I heard a hollow pop, like a bucket dropped into a well. Another pop and another. A sound I didn't recognize then. Ahead the grey Episcopal church with a narrow black spire stood back from the street. A dozen or more people collected around their cars in the parking lot. It was Sunday, and same as every Sunday people in suits and dresses headed inside. Bells rang in the spire.

When the bells fell silent, I heard a popping sound again as people in the lot and two groups parked up ahead on the street stepped out of their cars and swung the doors shut on their station wagons. Those who had parked on the street—I thought maybe for some reason these people weren't allowed to use the church lot, I didn't know—approached single file along the brick sidewalk. Three kids younger than me, four my mother's age, and two my grandparents' age. Each one looked up as they passed and seemed on the verge of telling me and my grandmother that we didn't belong here. No one said a word. I turned and watched them file through the church doors.

We passed York Hall, the largest house I'd ever seen, and continued down the hill with the river on our right. There was a breeze off the river that morning. I thought of Jacob perched above Boom Beach watching sheerwaters glide over swells and my grandmother standing outside the store on the island gazing west over the Minch. I looked downriver to see if the fog would roll in, but of course the fog didn't reach this far inland.

The riverfront oaks and maples towered higher than any trees I'd ever seen, except maybe in Bangor. It felt as if I'd traveled halfway around the world to get here, and I truly hoped the feeling that this town was a temporary port of call, somewhere you stopped on the way to somewhere else, meant we'd leave soon.

I did believe we would return to the island. I had the same feeling after a few years passed when we moved to another apartment up the street and my grandfather died. The same feeling a few years later when my grandmother died in her sleep. Now I'm almost old enough to collect my pension, but I sometimes still catch myself thinking I will move back to the island to my mother's house.

At the bottom of the hill, farther upriver than we had walked before, my grandmother stopped across from the old yellow house with the center stone chimney that someone fixed up a few years ago. The plank front door swung free and clanged against the clapboards. The corner posts leaned inward. The foundation had sunk. In the field, the branches of an apple tree sagged to the ground. By the water, someone had flipped over a skiff.

My grandmother crossed the field, and I followed her to the house where we both looked through a window at piles of leaves covering the floor of the parlor. A chair sat next to a far window facing the river, and I thought of all the people who'd lived in that house and sat watching ships sail toward the mouth of the river and the open ocean. Some of the sailors on those ships had returned, but many of them—more than I ever would be able to count—never saw the shore again.

Emily's Story

MARCH 4, 1810

This day baffling winds and black clouds ahead. Departed Outer-mark, District of Maine, at 8am. Filled away and ran on. At mid-night moderate. At 4am orders for the set up of the lee rigging.

MARCH 28, 1810

Father judged us to be abreast of Point Espada. Could not see the land. At midnight bore up across for Cape Tiburon. At 8am stood to the southard and shook reef out of the fore sail. About 10am saw 2 whales. We ran in to within 3 miles of the land and stood down.

APRIL 6, 1810

The crew is a poor, miserable set, and we have one man who fights with most every man in the fo'castle. He has pretended to be blind, crazy, and sick. Father thinks he is a queer fellow, and by his looks and appearance you would think he was fool-ish. But he can converse on any subject equal to any man on board. The men are all of the time peeking upon him, and if they would let him alone he would begin a quarrel with them. If they only point anything at him, he will swear and cry so you would think he was almost killed. He got his razor one night and pretended that he was going to cut his throat. Another time he went missing, and all hands were called up out of their berths. After looking the ship over, they finally found him down in the hole stowed away under some staves of cask. He pretended that he was afraid that some of the men were going to flog him. Another time he got to jawing with some of the men aft, and Father told him to go forward and stay there, so he went to the side of the ship and jumped overboard. All was excitement for a little while, for we did not know but he would drown at first, but I do not think that he had such a thought himself. He knew that the ship was not going very fast and that he could swim til the boat picked him up. He swam toward the boat like a good fellow until the boat got most to him and then he turned and went the other way and told us to let him drown. I do not think there is one aboard the ship but would be glad to get rid of him.

APRIL 10, 1810

Bore N.W. 12 mile L. obs Lon 18"18 74"20. Midnight moderate and fair, continued to tack near the shore. At 8am saw a small schooner in the offing and at 9am she passed under our lee and tacked and stood for us. The schooner was a quarter of a mile astern Cape Bona Maria bearing about S.E.b.S. 3 leagues. Tacked and ran to leeward of the schooner mentioned, who gave signs of his wish to board us but failing. Showed a blue flag with a yellow cross extending through it both ways. He then followed us near the shore when we were obliged to tack and ran before the wind to keep out of his way. He continued to chase us and set his square sail but could not come up with us. We hauled to the W.S.W., and he gave up the chase and steered along shore. Now, for the first time, he showed a large number of men. Father says that the ship was undoubtedly a pirate who wished to run us on board and that we are very fortunate.

MAY 1, 1810

The Cape of Good Hope. The wind blew hard, and the sea rolled mountains high. We did not know but our house on deck would go to pieces, but it stood yet. The galley went over one night, breaking the stove and everything that was in it, including two iron boilers and one large pot. The sea continued to rage with increased fury, and every wave seemed as if it would swallow us up. It roared so dreadfully that the sound is still running in my ears. I shall never forget that night. Mother and I stayed below and braced ourselves near the centre of the ship so we would not be thrown. Mother held my hand tight but showed no fear. I heard Father call to ready the axes to cut away the masts. At 12 we thought the tempest would abate, but it raged until 5am.

JUNE 2, 1810

Saw the land about Point Balasore and anchored. Father told me not to be so excited; we still have to take on a pilot and go upriver before we see Calcutta. I can't help it. Next morning the pilot got the ship underway, and we ran to the eastward into the middle channel. Passed several Indiamen lying at some distance from us in what Father calls Saugor Road. Father said that on this passage our distance run per log was 5800 miles. In going upriver to Calcutta, the first town was Kedgeree, a native village on the left bank. Two or three Europeans only reside here, Father said. We went ashore in boats made of bark sewn together, and I shall never forget the sensation I experienced when I first saw those dreadful-looking men entirely naked with the exception of a bit of cloth below the waist. The next day sighted Culpee on the right bank, a place similar to Kedgeree, and then finally Calcutta. The river opposite Calcutta was nearly a mile wide. In July, Father said, the river was so full that the freshes began, and they were sometimes very strong—so much so that vessels could not go against the tide even with favourable winds. The tide ran seven or eight miles an hour, down all the time, there being no flood or even still water. The air smelled of rotting clay and burning, the sky brindle. Father told me not to be so excited. He said I get too excited.

JULY 17, 1810

Father admires the 800-ton English ships owned by the East India Company. Our ship is less than 200 tons. After he said this, he then said, "We let out at the bung to stop the spoil." He wouldn't tell me what this meant. Mother said it was like pumping out the bilge. I asked her what that meant, and she asked me, "Why do we pump out the bilge?" And I said, "So we don't sink to the bottom." She thought she had answered me and went back to cooking. When she turned around and saw me still standing in the same place, she said, "Don't feel sorry for yourself. Go make yourself useful."

Father makes all his purchases of goods through his banian: sugar, ginger, raw cotton.

JULY 20, 1810

The streets are wide and straight in Calcutta, and men keep them wet all day long with buckets of water. Our house is brick, and we live on the second floor. Father's banian also lives in such a house, and his palanquin bearers rest outside when he is inside. We go to the English church, whose services are at 9am on Sunday. In the evening we walk on the esplanade that leads up to the fort. The trees are not large enough to make a shade, as they were planted a short time ago. People do not usually walk until near sunset, and the walk is covered with brick dust. People of the first rank are not seen there, according to my mother, but Father says he does not care. Many people live here in great style. Many men have their own palanquins—boxes on long poles—and wear white robes tied around their waists with no shirt at all. Six bearers form a set for a palanquin, and Father tells me they are all raised from a place called Baal. Some men also have carriages, but only the rich have Arab horses, which cost 3000 rupees.

Mother won't let me talk to a girl we met because she is Armenian. Her mother binds up her chin. I am also not allowed to talk to any of the dancing girls, who cannot talk to me anyway because we don't speak the same language. But they are allowed to drink spirits and live the way they want to. They attach gold and silver bells to rings they wear around their ankles. They also wear rings on their wrists and jewels on their ears and sometimes their noses. Mother says their motions are supposed to captivate men, and she tells me not to look, but I look anyway. They sing and wear no shoes, and their clothing, though brightly coloured and flowing like water around their bodies, barely covers their skin.

There are holidays all the time, and I never know when one will come along. Flags were carried through the street yesterday, and I ran outside to see a row of large elephants, each one carrying eight persons. Many more followed the elephants carrying temples and bright decorations, and their faces were filled with joy.

AUGUST 1, 1810

Father brought me with him to meet Captain John Dole of the ship *Golconda* from Newburyport, whom he had met before. A palanquin brought us there. It was my first time in one, and I was not sure that four men could carry Father and me, but he said it was no problem, and they did not seem burdened. We were met at the house by a Hindoo in full dress, who made a low bow. We went in and up a long flight of stairs, and the man left us standing in a large hall full of Hindoo servants in flowing robes and turbans of the purest white. I didn't see Captain Dole at first, but there he was on a lounge being fanned by one of the servants. We were soon outside and in a garee, a kind of carriage, and Father told me we were going to a linseed bazaar. I couldn't hear what Father and Captain Dole were saying. We turned off the main road and down a narrow lane. On one side there was a drain with putrid water and dead rats. Then we came to a huge storehouse full of linseed oil. The sun poured terribly on us for a long time as the linseed was weighed and Father and the men talked. I was faint, and at last one of the sircars sent a cooley after some fruit. He soon returned with mangoes, bananas, and something I thought was a melon. I could not eat the melon, but then I was shown to drink from one end. Green coconut milk.

AUGUST 9, 1810

Father, Captain Dole, and I went in his carriage to the Old China Bazaar. On the way, Captain Dole pointed out the burning ghaut where the Hindoo dead are burned, the dead house where the sick are brought to die, a Hindoo temple, the house of a Hindoo nabob, and the mint of the East India Company. We had to get out and walk because the English army was at the bazaar that day, and no sooner had we gone a few steps than I saw a man whose hand was the size of the bottom of a chair. He kept uttering "buck-shish" to Father and me, but Captain Dole told us to ignore him. Father threw a rupee at him anyway, and the man followed us, saying "deucerer" in my ear and waving his giant hand in the heat. We reached the bazaar only to come upon the crew of an American ship, just paid, who were having a knockdown. One man was horribly bruised with blood streaming down his face. He fell and did not hold out his hands. His head bounced when it hit the ground, and blood ran out into the dirt.

AUGUST 20, 1810

Father brought me to a festival at the edge of town called Churruck Poojah where we saw ladies in small temples held up high on sticks. At first he told me he would not bring me because it was not fit for a girl. Mother was against it. But I knew he would bring me as long as I did not tell Mother. He did not ask me not to tell Mother, but I knew I was not to. As we drew near, the air was thick with cooking, like cheesecloth soaked in hot butter. Thick crowds. There were dancing girls, almost naked. Father said the rich could eat as much as they wanted to. They kept filling their mouths. Music and smoke and singing filled the air of the streets and fields, and there was a sea of the poor, their skin covered with a few rags.

We came upon a large tank or pond overspread at fifteen or twenty feet high by a large net sprinkled with roses. There were several temples on boats floating there, as well as boats with dancing girls performing on the tank. Here there were so many people collected to see the show I felt I would be swallowed up. Father had to lift me up so I could see.

The most amazing sight was the torment some of the poor voluntarily suffered. They were encouraged by the priests,

according to Father. They displayed great pride and exultation. Some cut two gashes in each side of their bodies, about
two inches long, through which on each side they passed several strings twenty feet long. The ends of these were held by two
persons while the performer ran backward and forward along
the strings. Others passed a rattan through their tongues, constantly moving it up and down and running through the streets.
They were all attended by frantic music. A gentleman attached
to the Police Office told us that last year one of the natives held
a large snake in his hand. The snake suddenly cleared its head
from his grasp, entwined itself around the neck of the miserable man, and drew out his tongue. Some I saw with strings in
their sides looked no more than my age. Father said they were
wrought up with opium, which was why they were so exalted
and not in agony.

The most amazing and highest feat was the hook swinging.
An upright post was raised about twenty-five feet from the
ground, on top of which a crosspiece was placed on a swivel.
Hooks were suspended from one end, and from the other end a
rope reached to the ground, by which the crosspiece was moved
round. There were two hooks passed twice through the flesh,
one on each side about midway on the back, by which these miserable creatures were suspended twenty feet from the ground.
And they whirled round so rapidly as to bring their bodies in
a perfectly horizontal position, bearing entirely by the flesh so
hooked up. This continued fifteen or twenty minutes, yet no
sign of suffering was shown. On the contrary, they expressed
great exultation and exhorted to move around still more rapidly. Three of these machines were set up near to each other and
were constantly filled for several hours. The swinging man close
to us flew out and up until he was on the horizon and his chest
faced away from the centre. His eyes grew wide, and blood ran
down his back. Then the man's flesh broke, and he flew through

the air and hit the ground. Father turned me away before he hit the ground, but I heard him hit. It was like a sack of rice hitting the deck. On the way back to town, I saw one man had the marks of hook swinging six previous times. Father said they do this because they are Hindoos, but I could see that explanation did not satisfy him any more than it did me.

NOVEMBER 30, 1810

We left Calcutta drifting down with the tide for four days to six miles below Fultah. Moderate weather. The pilot left us. On October 1 crossed the Equator. On October 13 saw the land about middle points of Natal, according to Father. The 18th spoke again the ship *India,* a packet which we saw on our outward passage now returning from the Isle of Bourbon. Strong winds around the Cape of Good Hope. November 2 passed Ascension Island. 7th boarded by French Privateer. They tried to get Father to declare the cargo English, but he would not. They let us go. November 18 sounded on George's Bank, spoke several vessels outward bound. November 21 anchored Portland. November 30 at Outermark.

MARCH 4, 1812

In the country trade stopping at Bombay, Colombo, Tranquebar, Nagapattinam, Madras, and ports on the Malabar Coast. On arriving at Madras, the government boat came alongside. Father said first we would go to Fort St. George and Black Town. There was no harbour, so we had to anchor in the open road, exposed to the weather. There were 55 vessels anchored there. Loading and unloading all day. They wanted rice and pepper, and we brought Madeira, which Father said we were not supposed to have but did. We were to pick up Madras, Pulicat, handkerchiefs, blue guineas, carboys, nicanees, and punjum. We could not land our boats on the beach at Madras. After the Collector took his two and a half percent, they took our goods and us ashore in a government boat. The boats had their own caulkers, and the boats were made, Father told me, with no nails at all. They were sewed together, and we would soon see why, Father said. The surf was very high—higher than any surf I had seen from inside a boat or anything at Boom Beach in the worst gale. We had eight boatmen with us along with Father, Mother, and the casks. We rose up so high on the wave that I feared we would crash bow first and pitchpole. We landed flat so hard that my teeth banged together, and I thought they would fall out. All eight men in the boat jumped out at once and held the boat fast with ropes as the surf crashed over us and we were wet right through. One of the men lifted me straight out of the boat in his bare arms and carried me onto the beach. Another man carried Mother, who looked like a goose caught by the feathers being taken to the pot. Father took himself up the beach. When I looked back, I saw the men turn the boat on its side and dump all the casks into the surf. I did not think that could be right, but Father later told me that was how it was done. They rolled the casks forward through the surf and up the beach. And they flipped the boat back on its keel and shoved back out toward our ship.

MARCH 16, 1812

Madras. We walked up to the Custom House in Black Town, where the natives, Portuguese, and Armenians lived. The streets were narrow and dirty, and everything smelled of cooking fires and rot. The small buildings were made of mats. They were six or eight feet high, and a whole family seemed to live inside and look out at us. Their faces were very dark, and they had coarse dark hair, which grew long. Father told me many of the richer ones worked as dubashes. I looked for all three classes. The Gentoos did not shave their upper lip, and they wore a mark on the forehead—a single line. The Malabar shaved the upper lip and daubed over the forehead with something like blue paint. The Moor had no mark. And the Brahmin, the highest, would not touch the others without washing themselves. The lower classes wore nothing but cloth around their waists and small turbans on their heads. The next class up wore turbans, robes covering their bodies, and shoes. We saw no women in the streets at all. People ate yellow rice from large leaves. Same as in Calcutta, we saw Brahmins being carried in palanquins with two men in front and two behind. Many men came up to Father asking for fanams and "master's favour." Father said everyone here was a beggar if they were in the lower class. There was a man juggling four then five then six coloured sacks in the air. We came around a corner, and there was a camel surrounded by many people, and there was music, but I could not see where it came from. A man stepped out with a knife and slid it across the throat of the camel. The camel's tongue stuck out of its mouth, and its eyes grew large. Blood sprayed out over the people. Father led us away fast, and I did not see the camel fall to the ground. There were crows everywhere above. I could hear them above the music, and they swooped down looking for food but found none.

In the fort all the buildings in the middle of the square were tall and made of brick. It seemed like it would be a fine place to live, but Father said it would not be at all. There was an English church, which he said was the one good thing, and there was a large statue of Marquis Cornwallis. Father said that half the people in the world were born with saddles on their backs and the other half were born to ride those people to death. Mother asked why he came up with such awful sayings, and he said he had not. It was a saying from Montesquieu.

JUNE 9, 1812

There was a heavy gale of wind this morning, and we were scarcely able to keep our seats. By having one hand to steady the dish and another to hold the water, I was able to make one pudding. Mother in her zeal let the pan of dried apples go after being washed. A sea just struck the ship, which made her tremble and made me call out in fear. We were nearing the Cape about ten degrees more, and we should be steering north. We had a tremendous sea running in the latter part of the day. The highest I ever saw above the mast. We could carry but little sail with the ship pitching very heavy.

AUGUST 13, 1812

We saw giant pagodas. Father said they were 170 feet to the top. The largest was thirty feet square at the base, and then after fourteen feet there was a second story built on. Many of the natives gathered around us, but when we tried to enter they would not let us until we took off our shoes. Father did not want to take off his shoes. Our palanquins carried us to Negapatam, but once there we met the only English-speaking person and found him disagreeable. He did not offer us a seat in his own house. We left him and searched for lodging with one of the Dutch. One man offered us to stay with him in his apartments, but once we saw his premises we saw there was no prospect of repose there, and we set off back toward Nagore. Halfway back our palanquins began to complain loudly—they had not eaten in 18 hours. In the pitch dark, they set us down at a choultry—a hut made of reeds for the poor—and vanished. There are no public houses on the road. The people who travel the roads are too poor for public houses. We spent the night sleeping in our palanquin. In the morning, the bearers returned and took us back to Nagore.

SEPTEMBER 24, 1812

Heavy gale of wind blew us east all week, against the direction
we wanted to go. Mother was sick and vomiting after the first
day. Her illness was not because of the baby, Father said, as
it was not due for another many months. But Father worried
without saying so because of the other babies who did not live.
Father brought a goat this time, tied to the outside of the cabin,
in case it was needed to nurse the baby. Father said to pray for
calm seas and light westerlies.

OCTOBER 1, 1812

Another week of heavy gales. Mother could not swallow water
by the end. She throws up blood now.

OCTOBER 5, 1812

Mother died, and it fell to smolt October 2. Father did not come
out until after dinner. When he did come out, he fared poorly,
and I told him he had a brindle complexion and should be bedfast. He said for me not to concern myself about him, and he
said we had no choice but to bury Mother that day. Mr. Bunker helped sew her, which Father was loathe to do himself. Mr.
Bunker wrapped her in canvas and sewed the seam right across
her face. Father said one prayer. "Forasmuch as it hath pleased
Almighty God of his great mercy to take unto himself the soul of
our dear wife here departed, we therefore commit her body to
the sea . . . through our Lord Jesus Christ, who shall change our
vile body, that it may be like unto his glorious body, according
to the mighty working, whereby he is able to subdue all things
to himself." Father and Mr. Bunker hove her into the sea, and
her body sank fast because of the weight sewn into the canvas.

I write "her body" because it was no longer her. Afterwards, Father went to his bunk, and I went to mine. I know that Father does not place much stock in the Almighty—a habit he passed to me. Sometime in the night I woke to find him sitting next to me with a lamp. I hid my face so he wouldn't see how upset I was. He placed his hand on my shoulder and told me that she would want us to have courage and to go on without her. I knew he was right. There was nothing else to say.

DECEMBER 2, 1813

We took a severe gale from the North, were driven to sea again, and arrived in Vera Cruz nine days after. It is healthy here, as the climate is warm, the season is far advanced, and all is green and growing. The Perote and the Arazatio, with their snow-capped summits looking far above the clouds, appeared like watch towers upon the heavens. I never saw such mountains before, and I wished Mother could see them, although I thought better of mentioning this to Father. The people are with few exceptions of the Indian cast and hardy; they can live on a plantain a day. The city is built on a low sand plain. It is enclosed by a wall twelve feet high with five gates, and its streets are rather narrow, run at right angles. It is compactly built with buildings of brick or stone from two to four stories high, which are flat on the top and covered on the outside with whitish cement. There is a very handsome marketplace that is very well supplied with poultry, fish, vegetables, and fruits of a most excellent quality, but everything at an exorbitant price.

JANUARY 12, 1813

While spreading our clothes to dry, we saw above 40 Indians coming from the N.W. with bows and poison arrows. They came around us and seemed to be struck with our appearance, Mr. Bunker having 2 pairs of pistols and Father a double-barreled fowling piece, a pair of pistols, and a broadsword. Soon after giving them some rum mixed with water and some bread, we saw a company of Creoles and Indians coming back from the country. They proved to be the Commandant's people from Sin Jamaica. The Commandant said it was unsafe for us to remain on shore on account of the Indians and advised us to get our things again on board. Father said he trusted the mercy of the waves more than the ferocious savages. After much fatigue, we succeeded in getting most of our things in the boat with the Indians around us stealing whatever they could pick away. We prepared our guns by cutting bow ports and holding ourselves in readiness, suspecting an attack from the Indians the following night. They did not trouble us.

MARCH 20, 1813

I have been ill on the island these last months and not able to write. Grandma says I will be bedfast for months yet, and she plans to send me to Portland to stay with Aunt Gwen so I can see a doctor. I tell her that I don't need a doctor and that I want to be here on the island helping her with the house and the store. She tells me I am no help to her bedfast, and I believe what she says is true. I will go, but not because I want to.

MAY 14, 1813

I have been more ill these past months living at Aunt Gwen's than I was on the island, so Grandma was right to send me away. I would have been no use to her. And I have been so ill that Grandma would have come to grief to see me so bleak.

JUNE 30, 1813

Since I last wrote, I have made myself ready many times to say goodbye to this world. Father stayed with me through the month of June, but then he had to go. Twice the minister visited my bedside, and I prepared myself. In each case I was called back, and now I am able to sit up and read and write. Aunt Gwen is a saint, and as long as I live I will owe her my life. I know Grandma has been frightful for my state all these months. Aunt Gwen has not dared to tell her my true condition, but Grandma has a strong head and knows that I write when I can and that if I cannot write something is wrong. She wrote she was happy to get my last letter. I am yet on dry land, I dare say, and I feel as if nothing could do me in now. Aunt Gwen has a house full of books, and she has ordered me more books besides. I declare myself to be a fortunate soul.

AUGUST 29, 1813

Father was in a terrible fall the day before he was supposed to set sail. It was his intent, along with some others, to run the British blockage. He had a letter of commission from the government that allowed him to take British ships. It sounds dangerous to me and exciting. I knew they would not allow me to go with them. Before they set sail, he was in the rigging, doing a boy's job, which is like him, and his back hurt so badly that he could not get out of bed for a week. The co-owners of our ship, the Schooner Paris, were two brothers from Portland, and they said they would delay departure. My uncle John and my cousin Billy were meant to accompany Father. Father tells me I may never go again because the illness has left my lungs permanently weakened. I do not believe him.

SEPTEMBER 16, 1813

Father left with my uncle and cousin. They all came to Aunt Gwen's house to say goodbye, and all said they would see me again soon.

NOVEMBER 30, 1813

I had a letter from Grandma sent to me through Aunt Gwen. Grandma wanted her to give me the letter directly, and I soon saw why. Father's ship went down in October, and no one was found. It was coming winter when this news arrived, and I wished I were back on the island already to comfort Grandma. There was much to do at the store and to prepare the old house for the winter. For some weeks I thought of Father on an island somewhere, but I knew this was not true.

APRIL 10, 1815

I am back on the island now. Many ships have been in the harbour to purchase goods from the store, including a number in the coast trade and a few ships over 200 tons heading east: Brig Actor, Captain Elias Hunt; Schooner Poly, Captain Solomon Balch; Schooner Calais, Captain Christopher Pettingill; Brig Pilgrim, Captain Ebenezer Wheelright; Schooner Confidence, Captain Thomas Dodge; Sloop Friendship, Captain Josiah Toppan; Schooner Argonaut, Captain Micajah Lunt. At 8am cleared the Brig Actor and the Schooner Argonaut of their loads: 17,000 feet boards, 3,450 clapboards, 65 M' shingles, 7 blls pork, 750 Hoops, 50 blls Tar, 50 blls Flour, 50 shooks Hdds fish, bread molasses & a quantity of beef, some strawberries, onions & cabbages from the shore, powder, 48 HHds, 13 boxes Soap, 34 blls,

No 1 Beef, 10 blls, No 2 Ditto, 31 half Ditto, 39 Bxs Raisins, and 20 D. candles. Offloaded onto the Schooner Confidence 75 barrels of water, 10 barrels of flower, 5 barrels of salt beef, 1 salt pork, 1 sugar, 130 hogshead of salt, salt clams, and mackerel.

The Schooner Chance anchored at 6pm, and Captain John Soule reported that the Schooner Dover broke up last week on the Horse Shoals, no survivors.

Running In the Grass
1975

A PAIR OF NAKED FEET twitching and kicking through the high grass of Tarr's Field. Just the feet, a boy's ankles washed by the dew, the switching faint as the sound of a breeze through pine needles, the rhythm perfect and precise as if executed by a pianist's fingers. In the grass, he could run faster than the wind. In the grass, his feet hardly touched the ground at all. They seemed to move hundreds of miles an hour yet take days to cross a few yards. He might have passed into the trees and run straight out to sea, never to return, he was running so fast. When he reached the road leading to his grandmother's house, he tiptoed over the sharp rocks so as not to cut his feet.

Donna's Story
1980

D ONNA SAT BEHIND the counter in the store watching the
glare from the breakwater beacon sway in the harbor current. The harbor darkened at the heel of the day. The temperature was dropping, but her face still burned from talking to Gus
that morning. She laid her palm against the cold glass.

From the rocker by the stove, her grandson Corson snored
louder than her husband Phil. Rattled the boxes. Donna
would've been justified in waking him—the boy should sleep in
bed like everyone else—but she couldn't bring herself to do it.
Any sleep better than no sleep. She poked Corson on the shoulder, but the boy growled and nodded off again.

Her biggest worry was that there wouldn't be anything left
for Corson when he got older. She knew Gus feared the same
thing, but they sure went at their fears in different ways. Old
Gus, close to he didn't look so good anymore. She'd realized that
in his kitchen that morning. Splotchy cheeks. Hungover, probably. Still had a whiskey step. Probably needed to with that wife
of his, Flossie. Donna shivered at the thought of those white
scars on her hands from a childhood at the Dennis cannery and
a long nose that looked like it had been pulled off and put back
on in a hurry. Dogfish, kids called her.

She remembered when he married his first wife, Mary Lee.

Wedding in the church, suit and white dress, the minister from the *Sunbeam* pronouncing his full name: *Hector George Petingale Pinkham*. Two years later Mary Lee threw Gus out to live in his fish shack. So he ripped the plumbing out of the house. She covered his fish shack with blue paint and cut the legs off all his trousers.

That morning he'd told her that Danny had taken something from his son, Henry, but what did it matter? They'd always worked out their problems. Then it dawned on her that they were talking about the shit that Henry smuggled for the trawler.

Gus worked himself up to a big speech by scratching his beard. "I put up with a lot of shit from Danny over the years, Donna, since my sister left him with us, and I tried with him— you're not gonna tell me I didn't try."

"You should put him to work."

"I did!—you know that. There's a limit."

"I'm the one feeding him," Donna said. Danny was a Pinkham, but he was her child as surely as if she'd given birth to him. After his mother fled the island for the Main, Donna'd held him as a baby, fed him at her table. People who hadn't raised them as babies—and even some who had—didn't understand you always saw them in three-cornered pants. She'd only been able to have the one of her own. Not her fault.

"Even before this shit with Sarah, he was shacking guy's traps at night—using my fucking punt. I *bend*, Donna."

"You let your son bring that shit—whatever it is—onto the island from that West Indies trawler."

"They're not from the West Indies, the people on that trawler," Gus said. "Just the boat's from the islands—it's not even their boat."

Gus lowered his head, his bottom lip sticking out, and she remembered him as a red-faced boy, fishing from his first skiff. She had no business treating him like an idiot. That's what people on the Main did to everyone from the island. There was the story of Gus buying a toilet seat so his mother wouldn't have to scrape her nethers on a plank, and his father hanging it on the wall with an old picture of his parents inside. Not true. *They* started that story on the Main. She'd never let a single child on here winter with rags tied to their feet the way they once did over in the State of Maine not that many years ago. They weren't poor like those Queebs off the back road to Cutler. She felt sorry for the children in *those* places whether they got shoes or not. She wasn't sending Danny to live over there, even for a short time. That's what Gus wanted her to do.

As soon as Danny hit the Main, he'd give every dime in his pocket to the package store. And she wanted to say, but wouldn't stand to hear it, that he had other problems besides the brown bottle. The boy's thoughts moved sideways like a crab. He didn't know Donna's sister—no one did anymore. She left the island twenty-five years ago. The trees, roads, trucks, buildings on the Main all foreign—may as well send him to Vietnam, she wanted to say and was proud of herself for not saying because of Gus's younger brother, who took his last breath in some place called Ia Drang.

"I found this in the field." Gus reached for a blood-stained iron log dog from the counter and tossed it onto the table. "He was up there in the field killing my sheep with this while we sleep. Gonna be me next, or Sarah."

That was this morning, and she hadn't heard from him since. His boat was gone, so he was out changing the water on his strings and spinning himself into another fit of rage.

Jacob knocked on the door, startling Donna so badly she grabbed her chest. She'd told him a hundred times not to knock, just to come in like everyone else. Sometimes at the end of the day, he stopped by the store for a small box of Saltines, which he often finished before leaving. He had dark rings under his eyes and a few patches of scruff he'd missed on his neck. No doubt he'd worked all afternoon getting the school ready for the next day.

"Do you want me to lift him?" Jacob said as he put his crackers on the counter. "Carry him to your house?"

"Sit down first," she said. Jacob sat in the rocker next to the stove and sighed. Donna pointed at Corson. "The weather prophet needs his sleep."

"He's the best thing going," Jacob said. Donna could hear the island in his voice now, first time since he'd come back. He took a deep breath and yawned. Her daughter Rachel was a fool. Not only handsome, Jacob was from out there—or at least he'd *lived* out there. Yet Rachel didn't want him—didn't *think* she wanted him. Stupid girl didn't know what she wanted. Now Jacob was talking himself out of loving her.

Back before Jacob and his mother left the island twenty years ago, he and Rachel spent all their time together. Then one morning she woke up and went to school but couldn't find him. Stumped over to check on the falling-down shack where he lived with his mother and found no one but Jacob's father Everett passed out drunk in the middle of the floor. Rachel rushed into her back bedroom, now Corson's room, and closed the door. Donna brought her food, but she wouldn't eat. Brought her new shoes from Dennis, but she wouldn't try them on. Brought her books from Bangor, she didn't crack them open. Wouldn't come out except to sip water like a cat. Face like a plank. She was already skinny, her cheeks scooped like gutted quahogs.

Stoven came from a trip to the Main with a billy goat. No more than a boy himself, two years out the army, Stoven left the goat by Rachel's door. You couldn't separate her from that goat, which she tied outside the school and kept next to the counter while she worked the store.

Murdock, the goat, not a young man when he arrived, lived a

long life, another five years. In that time Rachel went after nearly every boy close to her age: Jeremy Coffin, before he joined the Marines, Bobby Neale, before he went fishing in Alaska, David Ross, Harold Beale, Nicky Fogg. All left the island. Boys who loved her and would've stayed if she hadn't treated them as if they were no odds to her. Fell for them on Monday, turned them upside down on Friday. Everyone was not Jacob.

When Murdock died a month after she turned seventeen, she sat on the end of the bed and cried. Didn't make a sound as the tears washed over her face.

"Listen," Donna said now to Jacob, "Danny might have to do just fine at my sister's place on the mainland."

There it was—she'd said it. Now it could be done.

"Are you sure?" Jacob asked.

"I'm not sure of anything. But the thing I want to say to you is don't give up on my girl. You came back to this island for a reason."

These men. No goddamned compass. If Donna hadn't married Phil, he'd have ended up with some saucepan from Manan and finished his days living like a slave to the Dey. She hoped Jacob was different.

"I don't think I've got to tell you I'm about all gone by," Donna added, "and it's gonna be up to you—you and Rachel."

"What're you talking about?" He sat up.

"Rachel'll be back from fishing soon and we're all gonna have to pull in the same direction. I don't think Rachel has the temperament for the store—but you do. And there's the boy."

Jacob's body seemed to shrink into itself, like a dog during a thunderstorm. He was still nodding when he said, "Do you think anyone can do what you do?"

"Me? I'm just some old lady." She'd never wanted anyone to think this way about her. She wasn't old and she wasn't a lady. "In a few years, I'll be dead anyway." No one could deny that much.

"I can't tell Rachel what to do," he said.

"Why not?" Donna rose to stand over him. Sometimes it was best to lie. "Rachel and the boy don't know their own minds," she said. The muscle under his eye twitched. No matter. Necessity would do the work of courage—a saying her mother often used.

"They need you right now, they both do. And you and Rachel love each other. Always have, always will. I know that better than the two of you. And the boy, Corson, he needs you." No lie there. He had no father of his own.

Jacob pulled in his lips. Jacob's mother, Sarah Ann, had said in a letter to Donna that she worried about her son. Sarah Ann hadn't heard from him since he first landed back on the island several months ago. Donna hadn't written back yet. She didn't want to mention Jacob growing thinner every day. Donna fed him, but worry picked like a seagull at his flesh when she wasn't looking.

Sarah Ann said she'd been praying for her son. Apparently, they had God in Arizona, but Sarah Ann would remember that the church boat only came once every two months, less in the winter. Sarah Ann would remember that the island took Donna's grandfather at thirty-five and her father, drowned off the Motions. Sarah Ann would pray for her son to get on his knees and submit, but any mother living on the island could only wish the opposite for her son. You didn't submit out here.

Jacob removed his shoes, and his long bony feet rested on the worn floor in front of the stove. He loved her daughter and grandson. Jacob was as stubborn as Donna herself. Any man you could reason with wasn't worth a hole in the snow anyway. True of Jacob, true of her brother, who'd grown up standing at the breakwater shading his eyes so he could see the thin green line of the Main where there was no beginning, no end, no marks to measure yourself against.

Donna understood. At eighteen, she went down to Orono
where all the girls she knew from the island married or worked.
Planned to follow her mother and grandmother and study to
become a teacher or a nurse at the U. But one year felt like a
decade. Every day she walked by dozens of faces she'd never
seen before. Shared a room with a girl who called out for her
dog, Buddy, every night and filed her nails at six in the morning
before breakfast.

Whatever Jacob'd left behind in the West didn't matter now
that he was here. You couldn't summon the force to stay unless
you had first left. Life had to break you. The island had once
bred people who'd ranged to every gunk hole of the earth.
Her own grandmother, born in the middle of a typhoon in the
Indian Ocean, carried the wind in her eyes until her last hacking cough.

Jacob wiped his eyes and leaned forward to rest his hand on
her arm. She thought at first he gazed at the floor because he
was embarrassed for himself, but then she realized her own
eyes were a bit wet.

"You want me to lift him up?" Jacob said, and Donna said yes
if he could. Corson was a skinny thing for his age. Jacob hefted
the boy into his arms. With Corson's head balanced against his
chest, they climbed the trail to the house. Jacob didn't know yet
he was no coward. He'd find out. His pant leg rode up his calf.
Donna reached out before he took another step and pulled the
cuff down.

Halfway up the trail, Jacob stopped. Due west, deep swells
cut in half by the prow of the island rejoined and continued
toward the Main. In the darkness, two lights—bridge lights—
rose and sank from view in the trough of a swell.

"You think it's them, the trawler? Or someone else?" Jacob
asked in a hushed voice, trying not to wake Corson.

"Them." The West Indies trawler—or wherever the hell they

were from. "Goddammit," she muttered and slapped Jacob on the back to hustle faster toward the house. Inside, Phil slept in his chair. Donna reached under the bed in her room and took out Phil's hunting rifle while Jacob set Corson down on the sofa. She shoved a box of cartridges into Jacob's hands and told him to follow. They stalked the harbor trail to the breakwater and picked along the slippery rocks. Jacob said careful and she said keep up. Maybe the trawler lights would vanish by the time they reached the halfway mark. A blessing, but she also wanted her chance. The mist and spray wet her cheeks, and she tasted salt as she searched the distant black folding over black. The open mouth of the Minch.

"Give me the box," she said and quickly loaded the shells. Then the bridge lights appeared. Slamming the bolt in place, she took aim at the light and fired. Cleared the case and fired again. And again, and once more after the light vanished.

"You think they're gone?" Jacob asked.

"No."

"Down in the trough."

"Yuh."

She fired into the darkness where the light had been. When the light appeared four points to the southwest, she kept firing, reloaded, fired again until the light beat south making ten knots. Resting the butt of the rifle on her knee for a moment, she took another breath and thought to hand the stock to Jacob, who cradled it in his arms like a child.

"I think they got the message," Jacob said.

"What message?" Donna turned around to see the lights of the houses on the harbor and in the woods burning. Corson, Phil, and Danny stood in the kitchen window. Some of the fishermen hung around the store.

As she and Jacob walked by, she was glad she'd given the gun to him. Just as well everyone thought he'd fired the shots. Only when they entered the kitchen did she take it back, clear the chamber, and shove it back under the bed. Phil sank into his seat and relit his pipe.

"Jesus, Donna," he said under his breath. "That's a fierce invitation."

"What was it?" Corson asked.

"No reason for any of you to get up from your naps," Donna said.

Corson followed her around the house, but by the time Donna fed the stove and put the pot on, his eyes had grown drowsy again. She went for firewood behind the house where she needed to swallow half a dozen cold, deep breaths to chase away the sudden feeling that her heart would stop. The stars pricked at her eyes.

Inside, she found Phil asleep with his pipe smoldering in his lap. Jacob and Corson lay on opposite sides of the sofa.

Donna retrieved a quilt and blankets from the chest, one for Phil, one for Corson, one for Jacob and one for Danny, who had curled up like a dog on the floor in the corner.

The Milkshake
1969

DONNA THOUGHT OF a story, a cruel one to tell, about what had happened with Danny at the Wilson's in Dennis when he was younger, and she took a bunch of the island kids to the Main for shopping. Danny wandered off by himself with his frappe, and after all this time, she couldn't remember why she didn't go after him. She never let him go off by himself on the Main. Maybe she was tired that day. She saw the fight as she ran down the street too late. Lawrence Robinson, who owned Wilson's Drugs and coached the Dennis basketball team, ran out, pulled the two Dennis kids off Danny. That should've been it, but Danny rose to his feet, flew into the Wilson's, lifted one of the big racks, and heaved it through the plate glass window. Out came cough syrup, bandages, books, copies of the paper, and bottles of Coke that popped when they hit the pavement. Danny puffed out his chest in the hole where Wilson's had been painted across the window. On the sidewalk, he clutched a piece of broken glass in his fist. Lawrence tried to catch him. Only when Donna said Danny's name did he come to her. The bird's nest of his hair.

The Chicken Story
1977

PATRICIA GOOCH was purchasing a container of milk from Donna Wills at the island store. Donna asked how she was doing. Patricia had no children, and she had lost her husband the year before. She reached up to tighten the scarf that covered her head. No one on the island could remember seeing Patricia without her scarf. Even when she sat at home, she would not take it off. Only at night would she take off the scarf, but no one knew about these scarfless nights except Patricia herself. She had grown up on Manan Island, then married Steven Gooch from Outermark Island. When Steven drowned off Machias Seal Island in a storm, she was left alone.

Patricia rested her milk down on the counter and stared at Donna and Donna's grandson, Corson, who was writing the price of the milk in the charge account. Patricia rarely spoke to others.

"I suppose you're wondering about that chicken out front?" Corson said to Patricia. Corson kept a chicken in a crate in front of the store. The chicken had grown to full size but had never possessed feathers. Patricia simply stared back at Corson and blinked her eyes three times in quick succession. "Do you think that chicken came into life with no feathers like that?" Corson asked Patricia, who saw no reason to respond. She knew it was

possible to live on an island and not have already heard everything someone wanted to tell you, but she recognized a trick
question when she saw one.

———————

Earlier that summer an unknown writer named Alexander
Vonderlin had arrived on the island asking for a place to rent.
There was only one empty place where anyone could sleep and
that was above Donna's store, and it was not for rent. Alexander's parents had died long ago, and his sister had just died in
childbirth. He had never been married and had worked at any
number of different jobs. He had decided recently to become a
writer and had come to the island to find inspiration in isola-
tion. He was interested in failure and the truth. Donna had a
stack of debts she would never be able to pay, so she welcomed
this man, strange or not, who introduced himself as a writer
and produced a roll of money from his pocket. He claimed to
know the summer resident on the island people called Christopher Columbus, who had given him a ride to the island and who
was himself strange but harmless. Christopher Columbus had
a boat, but he didn't know anything about boats. Lobstermen
from the island frequently came to his rescue.

Alexander didn't stay on the island for long, but that's all right
because he didn't really come all the way out to the edge of the
continent to find inspiration, or if he did, he was clearly fooling
himself. As he sat upstairs with the pen poised above the paper,
Donna stood at the counter of her store thinking about the man
upstairs and what he might be doing.

The writer had brought with him a small wooden crate.
Donna had assumed that the crate contained books, a natural
companion to the writer's life, but she had started to wonder if
he was actually a drug dealer or a satanist.

One day Eddie Boynton came down the hill to the store. That day he had huge circles under his eyes, and so did Donna because people on the island were sick and cold already, even though the winter hadn't even started yet.

Eddie pointed to brown liquid seeping down through the ceiling and onto the floor by the cooler. She turned and watched the dripping. Eddie's brother Larry showed up and asked about the writer. Everyone had heard about the writer.

"That's not a good sign," Larry said, pointing at the brown liquid.

Larry had a crooked jaw and was a bearded man with arms the size of trees, while Eddie looked like a violin that had been used in a rock band. Violet, Eddie's wife, who showed up to look for her husband, was constructed of sharp, gray edges. When she breathed, she made a sound like a lobster boiling in a pot.

After the first snow, Alexander retuned to the mainland with Christopher Columbus. No one ever saw Alexander again.

———

The one thing to know about Patricia is why she always wore the scarf on her head. It was because she pulled her hair out. Even in her sleep she reached up to the top of her head and pulled out clumps of hair until her scalp bled and her neck and sheets turned red. Underneath her scarf, the scalp was bruised, torn, and scarred. What little hair remained grew in clumps. The one and only thing Patricia knew about herself was that she pulled her hair out. She did not want to reach her hand up above her shoulder and yank, but she had no choice. She wasn't afraid that she would never be able to stop, but she was afraid that someday there would be no more hair to pull out.

Putep
1727

Captain Robert Cushing, Eastport, Province of
Massachusetts, to Lt. Gov. Dummer, Boston, Massachusetts,
November 27, 1727.

I writ to you September 14 last bout the island Outermark
the Tribe call Putep. Myself and John Wills has a fishing station
and bilt a stone house there. I must also aquaint you about ye
currant 10 Days Past, 12 of the tribe wear over to Putep Island to
kill Sils but finding not any & being Detained ther Sunday Day
by wind & wether they Lit of a Cow & hoggs belonging to John
Wills and myself which they Kild & must Pay for. On ye second
of this Inst, Indian named Louis, his two sons were here. One
of them owned he had killed three piggs there, tho at first they
denied it, & I saide nothing to them about paying, so neither did
they say anything, only that they were all so poore they would
have died if they had not killed them.

Lt. Governor Dummer, Boston, Massachusetts, to Capt.
Robert Cushing, Eastport, Province of Massachusetts,
Dec. 13, 1727.

Dear Sr, I Reed your Letter of the 27th last And I am much Dis-
pleased at the Action of the Indians at Putep in Killing the Crea-

tures there; Upon which Occasion You must Inform the Sachem & other Chief men as well as the immediate actors as follows. That I very much Resent this Liberty they have taken in Killing the Creatures which belong to John Wills and yourself which is contrary to the Articles of Peace And that Common Justice which the English and Indians owe to one another, Not to Hurt one another in their Just Rights and Properties; Which Fault is much aggravated from the Constant Care I have taken to have them supplied with all manner of Necessaries at the Trading Houses: And as it was one View I had in this free & Generous Trade which I have carried on with them, To prevent such ill practices from them, So I flattered myself it would have that good Effect; And that as Justice & Honesty are the surest Methods to preserve the Peace, so, on the Contrary Violence & Robbery have a direct tendency To disturb ye friendship & good Agreement which I have Endeavored to maintain with the Indians & which I hope will subsist between us & them to the latest Posterity: That if they have not already made full satisfaction for the damage done, I expect They do it without delay, And that I insist upon it that their Chiefs do frequently warn all the Young Men That They never Meddle with any of the English Cattle or other things belonging to them: And that I expect They will make strict inquiry whether this Action was done through Rashness and Wantonness or by the Instigation of Such as are both theirs and Our Enemies, the French, who may have a wicked Design to make a Misunderstanding between us; And that in this and all other the like Cases They do Exemplary Justice to the Offenders, in order to deter others from Doing the like Mischief. This is what you are to say to them. No more at present from Your Humble Servt.

Sachem Louis to Lt. Gov. Dummer, Boston, Massachusetts,
Dec 21, 1727.

Brother you did not hearken to us about the Englishman on
the Island Putep; he hurts us in our sealing and fishing. It is
our livelihood and others too for what we get we bring to your
Truckmasters. We do not hinder him from fishing, but he does
not belong there. The island belongs to us. If you don't Remove
him in two months we shall be obliged to do it ourselves. We
have writ to you before and have had no answer. If you don't
answer we shan't write again, as it is our custom if our letters
are not answered not to write again.

We salute you and all the Council on behalf of the Passamaquoddy Tribe.

Arnold Green, Eastport, Province of Massachusetts, to
Lt. Governor Dummer, Boston, Massachusetts, Feb 10, 1728.

There has a very Bad affair happen'd here (as I'm informed).
There are Two Indians killed on Putep Island. One Wright came
up & informed Capt Lithcow of it & Said he knew the Two men
that saw it Done—& help'd to bury them there, & Their Guns,
but he wou'dnt tell their names who done it. I know them to be
John Wills and his sons William and Corson Wills who had been
ordered off by agreement with Massachusetts and the Tribe
under the prev Gov and Treaty. The Indians are ignorant of it at
present. But when they know it, they will revenge themselves,
I am afraid, & we may Look out for we are but Weak. If this be
true, I think, Such Villains ought to dye without pity. Another
report stated that John Wills burned the grass on Howard Island
near the Main, in order to improve the hay crop for his use. The
Tribe warned him to desist, which he refused to do.

Captain Robert Cushing, Eastport, Province of
Massachusetts, to Lt. Gov Dummer, Boston, Massachusetts,
May 29, 1728.

To the Hon'ne his Majesty's Councill: May it Please Your Honours, I thought ye Accot Inclos'd of the Destruction of the John
Wills Family at Putep wou'd be significant to Your Honours and
therefore have inclos'd it as I just now took it from the mouth
of ye Young Lad William that made his Escape, the son of John
Wills. The 6th Inst in ye Night there came ten or twelve Indians
on Putep Island, on Tuesday Morning they attempted to breake
open the Wills House, but Wills perceiv'd them and knocked off
a board from ye Roof, to prevent the firing the House. Some of
them were Endeavoring to do at ye same Time, and Wills and
Richard Boynton and son fir'd thro' a Loop Hole and said he
had kill'd One, but they return'd ye Fire, and so continued ye
Engagement till Thursday following about 12 o'clock, when as
Wills and Boynton were raising their Heads over a sort of Breast
work they had prepar'd for ye Purpose to get a shot at ye Enemy,
they sent a Ball through his Head and kill'd him dead on ye
Spot, wounding Boynton, & then Wills' wife call'd out for Quarter, whereupon Wills' son who gives this Accq jumpt out over
ye wall of ye House and Hid in the woods, and thereby Escapt
and ye Indians Killed Boynton took said John Wills's Wife, and
Boynton's wife and five Children and Carry'd them off; the Next
Day ye Young Lad William Wills that gives me this Accq says
he paddled about two Leagues off in the Bay in a Float, and was
taken up by a small Fishing Schooner belonging to Brunswick.
The next Day a Saturday, the said Schooner Went on Shoar on
the Island & found said John Wills scalpt, and bury'd him, this
Young Lad is about sixteen Years Old & says they kill'd several
of his Father's Cattle Empty'd ye Fether beds and carry'd off
ye Ticken and every thing Else they cou'd in said Wills fishing

Boat, he further says that ye Indians set fire to crops and buildings and fire spread over the whole island. A day or two after
his Father was Bury'd, the Skipper he was board of went into
Madumpkook where the Indians had Engag'd one Jacob Elwell's
House in ye Night sot fire to it, but a sudden Rain put it out. I
Fear more such Occurrences will follow. John Wills's wife and
younger son Corson Wills and Daughter were taken into Captiv-
ity upriver. Here the mother was separated from her children.
She was taken through the Wilderness to Quebec where Captain Watkins paid her ransom. She sailed hence to England and
to Falmouth. The wherebouts of Corson Wills are unknown.

Mary Wills, Gorham, Province of Massachusetts,
to Lt. Gov. Dummer, Boston, Massachusetts, October, 1728.

To the Hon'ne his Majesty's Councill, I Humbly sheweth That
in the Month of March the Indians beset the House where my
Husband and I lived at a place called Putep known too as Outermark in Which we resolutely defended for Several Days but
on the Tenth day of said Month my Husband was killed, the
House broken up & rifled, your Petitioner and two Children
carried away Captives. One son escaped. I was Seperated from
the Children and have not seen nor heard any Thing of Corson Since; from Passamaquoddy your Petitioner was carried to
Quebeck where having tarried some time, I interceded with one
Capt. Watkins a New England Gent to pay my Ransom, which
he did, to the best of remembrance Two Hundred and about
Fifteen Livres, then I took Passage for England, from thence to
Falmouth & thence to this Place having undergone great Hard-
ship during this Time. Your Petitioner is now called upon for
her Ransom Money, and having nothing to pay it with, nor any
where to put her Head, nor any Thing to Subsist on I Humbly
beseeche the Compassion of your Excellency & Honours, that

said Ransom Money may be paid by the Province, and your Petitioner also granted such further Relief as to your known Wisdom & Goodness shall seem met—And as in Duty bound will ever pray.

Anne Wills Neale of Bangor, Maine, to Charlotte Wills
of Portland, Maine, August 13, 1930.

Dear Mrs. Wills, my daughter spoke of you the other day and said she met you in Portland. You are a teacher and she is a teacher, she says. She also tells me you are a cousin. Maybe she mentioned to me how many times removed, I can't remember. She may have mentioned to you that I am 83 years old this month, so I don't take in new information the way I once did. If she says we are related, I am sure it is true. She has become interested in the history, and I am glad of it. My daughter tells me you were asking about Outermark and Corson Wills, one of the early settlers of that island, who I am told is our common ancestor. In fact, I grew up in a house he was said to have built in the middle of the island. I lived on Outermark until I met my husband and moved here to Bangor. Corson lived a long time ago, so of course everything I know of him came from my grandmother Anne, who talked about him to me when I was young. I have a document handwritten by my grandmother about Corson's experiences when he was young. The story must have been told to her at some point, and she wrote it down in case she forgot. My daughter has typed up a copy of the document, which I have included in this envelope. As you may already know, Corson Wills was the son of John Wills, the first member of our family to live on the island. He was what they called a squatter, I believe. No one was living on the island, so he and another man began to fish from the island and keep cows there. The Indians, I believe, used the island for fishing in the summer and were not happy about his presence there. Corson and his sister and mother were taken captive from the island in 1727 or so.

My daughter has always loved to be out in the world meeting new people, so I am happy that you two have made a connection. The older she gets, the more interested she is in the past. I confess the opposite is true for me.

Corson Wills, 1712-1782, his story as told by Anne Wills.

Corson, his sister Sarah, and their mother Mary were placed in canoes at Outermark in 1727 and taken to the mainland. There they were unloaded and marched east with their captors through the woods until they came to the outskirts of a village, where they were tied to trees. The warriors watched the harbor until the men left to fish. Then they killed a man and took more captives in the village. At another village, several parties gathered and Corson was almost sold to a Jesuit, who offered pieces of gold for him. His mother said that she would rather see him into the grave than see him sold to a Papist.

Separated from his sister and mother, Corson travelled up a river with a small group, and at one point he found himself in the middle of a dance. Women kicked and yanked his hair and cut him with shells. Several women pulled him into a wigwam filled with yelling and dancing. At the center of the crowd stood four other captives, three boys and a girl. Several grabbed one of the boys by the arms and legs, flung him up in the air and slammed him repeatedly on the ground until blood gushed from his mouth and the back of his head. A woman and a girl took Corson's hand, and he thought he would be next, but they led him out of the wigwam and half a mile away to the home of a Frenchman and his wife. They fed Corson instead of killing him.

Next day he headed north by canoe in a group of eight Indians, one of whom acted as Corson's master. When the river iced
over, they pulled the canoes out and continued on foot over the
land or on the ice. Sometimes they walked four days without
eating. When they killed a moose or sometimes a bear, one of
the women would sing.

Corson and his party encountered a large group of Indians
who had lost a number of people to a party of English, who were
paid in sterling by the Massachusetts government for Indian
scalps. The new group had two captives of their own secured in
a wigwam. They grabbed Corson and threw him in the middle
of a circle and beat him with sticks and the butt ends of axes for
most of the day until he could not walk. Again he thought he
would die, but he did not. He and his small group returned to
the woods and at one point the temperature dropped so low that
he fell down. The women built a fire and took off his moccasins
and mittens. His feet and ankles had swelled and turned black
with blisters. He had begun to understand some of their language and heard an argument arise about whether he would die
or not. An older woman thought they should leave him because
his feet would rot. But soon his feet warmed by the fire, and the
black crust fell away like a leather shell. Only the ends of his
big toes remained black. One of the Indians gave him a knife
and told him to cut his toe off at the first joint, which he did.
They gave him rags and fir balsam to bind his feet but said he
would probably die anyway. Using two sticks he pushed himself
through the woods until he collected more balsam, which he
heated in a shell over the fire and applied to his ankles and feet.
Within a week he could crawl around on his hands and knees.
The woman who had said they should leave him behind sewed
two wooden hoops to his feet, which allowed him to walk on his
heels in their tracks. Several times he fell through the snow or

through ice into water, and the excruciating pain knocked him out. By the Grace of God, as he put it, he either rose again or one of his group helped him stand.

When his master died of an infection that started after he cut his hand on a branch, another argument arose about what to do with him. Two people in the group claimed him, while another suggested they end the argument by killing him. The woman who had suggested they leave him behind when he froze his feet said they should sell him to the French. A year and a half after his capture, the group sold him to the captain of a French ship, who sold him, four months later, to one of Corson's uncles living in Vaughn on the Kennebec. Corson lived and was eventually reunited with his mother. His younger sister Phoebe, who had followed a different route to Quebec, was ransomed a year later but then returned to the tribe she had lived with. At eighteen, Corson returned to Outermark to rebuild his father's house there. Corson married Patience Ingersoll from Grand Manan Island, and had three boys, one named Corson, who was my great grandfather.

Donna Wills Cushing, Outermark Island, Maine to Catherine Wills Spires, Appleton, Maine, September 17, 1955.

I am writing this letter in haste and having Phil take it to the Main to post as soon as I finish because I want you to hear from me and not someone else that Pa passed yesterday afternoon. I must prepare you for the circumstances of his passing, but I do not know how to do so. In the year since you last saw Pa, he aged a whole lot, or so it seemed to us. At the same time, he was only sixty, which is not old for the men in his family. When I say that he seemed to have aged in the last year, I don't mean physically. He looked the same, straight up and down. Every day last winter he was after working on his gear in the fish house, same as ever, but this season he decided not to fish. He looked the same but wasn't the same. He wouldn't look at you, which wasn't like him. At the end of the summer, he hauled his boat. Said she had a leak.

He rarely crossed over to the Main with us for any reason. If he needed something from Dennis or Bangor, I got it for him or Phil did. Yesterday he decided he would come with us on the mail run. I was along to buy supplies for the store, and he seemed upset that I had decided to go. He didn't say a word the whole way across, just sat on the bench by the helm. In town he walked to the diner and bought a milkshake the way he always did for all of us in the summer when we were kids. Then he went to the bank, which I thought was strange. He never went to the bank. He kept his money hidden in the house, as you know. By the time I returned to the boat with my supplies, he was sitting next to the helm with his hands in his lap. For a moment there he reminded me of our brother, when he was a boy. While we waited for Phil to arrive with the mail, I asked him why he'd wanted to come with us that day. "Felt like it," was all he said. Cloudy and mizzling on the way in, it was thick of fog and the sea rolling back across the Minch.

Ten miles out, where the current rips, he stood up as if someone had pulled him to his feet from above. I noticed his pockets were weighted down. I couldn't tell with what at first until I remembered his trip to the bank. A roll of pennies fell from his pocket and broke open on the deck. I thought he would scoop them back up. You know how near he was. Instead, he walked the length of the boat and stepped off the stern.

We turned around and searched. Starting in circles where I'd seen him go over, we widened the circle until we had covered an area the size of the island. There was no sign of him, Catherine. The fog rolled in thick and the light failed. All we could see was the compass. We were lucky, on a night like that, to find the lights of the harbor.

Jacob's Story
1980

JACOB LEANED AGAINST Danny's shack at the harbor and watched waves travel west like hands beneath a sheet. On days like this in Tucson, heat rolled over the Sonoran hills where people died of thirst trying to cross from Mexico. Here on the island, the ocean stretched farther than the desert and the light seemed made of ice. You could die of a different kind of thirst out here. Too much water, too much salt.

Rachel was out there diving near East Rock. Days on the bottom combing for urchins. She'd told him that most of her dreams were underwater—an hour on the surface felt like a day, while an hour underwater seemed to pass in minutes. She had said she would be back today by three. It was past five now. He kept looking to the west, waiting for the high white Novi bow to split the horizon. She would only stay for a night before heading out again to dive in Muscongus Bay.

Jacob started walking back to Rachel's house in the middle of the island. He'd wait for her there—if she came back at all. In the field, he stopped to listen to the surf crashing on Boom Beach. The clouds had burned off. To the east, wave crests angled against the sunlight and the ocean ignited. Surf fanned spray across his lips. Licking the salt, he tasted a mixture of earth and low tide. He'd stood in exactly this spot countless times before.

Ever since he and his mother left the island twenty years ago, he'd been waiting for his life to start. He went to college; met Michelle and her daughter, Sierra; trained as a surveyor; and worked all over the world. Now he was back here, standing about 10,000 feet from the harbor. Measuring distance over land, there was no real straight line on the island or anywhere else, only the most direct route into a jungle, through valleys and forests and villages, across rivers and ranges, and sometimes right through the sides of hills. His secret then, still his secret now: he could go and go, twenty hours a day, more. He could burn each day down to the stump. Nothing left. Sleep a black hole he fell into. The oil people needed a man like him—useful. But you couldn't measure anything that mattered. No map could take you to when you'd started.

Now he saw the island through double vision—through the eyes of the boy he remembered and through the eyes of the man who stood on the outside of these people's lives looking in. Both visions were false, which meant he lived nowhere on any map.

His father hadn't been from here, and people had never accepted him. Part Acadian, part Passamaquoddy (like Danny's father, Donna said), part local kid from Dennis, he hadn't belonged on the Main either. His father's mother, from somewhere east of Lubec, fell in briefly with one of the Ingersolls from Dennis. She raised his father on her own, working at the fish plant. So the story went.

When Jacob first got off the bus on the mainland six months ago, he checked into the motel on the edge of Dennis and walked around. He didn't have a plan. As he pulled up to the island wharf a few days later, riding in Phil's boat, a boy in jeans ran out of the store. Donna stumped down the wharf after him.

"Jacob," Donna said with a smile. Donna led them into the store. Same tilted steps painted red, same click to the latch as the bell clanged. He stepped over the threshold and a wave of stove heat drew him toward the center of the store. The same spindle chair sat beneath a strip of fly tape. "Sit down," Donna said, "and rest your hands and your feet." Tea had been simmering on the stovetop. He took a cup from her and settled into the chair. She placed a stack of Mary Anne's on an upturned wooden crate next to him. Woodsmoke, must, salt. The floors creaked. The boy, called Corson, sat behind the counter and tracked his every move.

When Rachel showed up outside the store and saw him, she stared at his face without changing the blank expression she must've been wearing all day. Might've been wearing for twenty years. When they were young, they'd talked of how their lives would be when they were old living on the island with children of their own.

Jacob saw her thoughts spinning behind her eyes, though what she really thought and felt had always been buried like a fossil inside a stone.

"Come on," Rachel said without looking at him and started up the road toward the middle of the island. Jacob followed and Corson stayed put with his hands on his hips. Twenty yards along, Rachel stopped and raised an eyebrow at his boots—western boots, not something anyone would wear around here. He was more worried about what she saw in his face. He hadn't shaved in a week, hadn't brushed his teeth that morning.

"So you're a cowboy now?" she said and watched him with the eyes of a customs official.

"I should've written that I was coming," he said. He didn't want to say the truth—that he'd boarded a plane, then a bus, then saw Phil, all without being sure what he was doing or why. He had inched closer but hadn't been sure the whole time how far he wanted to go. Didn't know why he was even here after being gone for twenty years.

Up the road, they passed Gott's house, where the branches of old apple trees hung in the knee-high grass. The last time he'd seen it, the Gotts had been living there. He stopped walking and stared at the gap where the front door had been.

"What's the matter?" Rachel asked.

For a moment it felt as if he was still thirteen, and everything they passed—the Neale and Fogg houses, empty now with broken windows and peeling roofs—seemed to have changed overnight. "What happened? Where did people go?"

Rachel shook her head. He wanted to ask about the boy he'd just met, Corson, but was afraid to hear Rachel say she was married. He found himself trying to track her mood by catching glimpses of her face. The constant flight of her thoughts pulled him in her wake. He didn't feel a day older than the last time he'd seen her. He followed her lead to the field above Boom Beach, where spray from the crashing waves drifted through the grass. When a swell washed over the white granite at one end of the beach, the water turned emerald in the sunlight. It felt as if the ocean had opened its eye to look at him.

Rachel turned to him. The lines high on her cheekbones and around the corners of her mouth seemed to grow out of the girl he'd once known. Her face rose to the surface; even the way she stood on one hip matched a pattern etched in his memory. He kept staring at her until she laughed and shook her head.

"Here you are," she said. "Out of nowhere. Did you think I would be the same?" Behind her, a group of kids with Corson at the front advanced like an army across the field. Out of sync, slowing, girls light on their feet, another boy in the back kicking the ground. When Rachel shooed Corson with her hand, Corson turned and bolted across the field, the black soles of his feet snapping in the air. Halting at one of the apple trees, he jumped up and hung from a branch. Rachel grabbed Jacob's arm and leaned over. "Come on," she said, "they're just gonna keep on us." The smell of dried hay mixed with her sweat struck like a match in his chest. He followed her across the field, the cold wind croaking in his ears. By the time he reached the house where she'd grown up, his heart pounding, he knew he would find a way to stay here with her. After screwing up so badly with Michelle and Sierra in Arizona, he was getting another chance.

She pushed open the door. In the kitchen where he'd sat with her and Donna and drank tea by the stove in the winter when he was young, she leaned back against the wall and let her arms fall at her sides. Her mouth opened. Her breath brushed his cheeks. In one motion, he stepped over the years he'd lived in Arizona, and pressed his lips to her neck. He hadn't so much traveled through time as erased it.

The six months that had passed since his first day back on the island now felt like years. He glanced across the field at the school, the only space on the island that had felt like his. Temporarily his. He was no teacher. Windows on each side of a red door, brick chimney in the center. Warped panes. He'd spent most of the last ten years working outside. Now he came to the school every day and stood in front of ten kids from seven to seventeen. For some reason, they mostly did what he asked them to do. They mostly listened to what he said.

His first day on the job, one of the kids stood in front of the school in his jeans and rubber hip boots. Cocky, covered in fish scales, he'd come in from fishing with his father 60 miles out. He looked at Jacob with obvious scorn, as if Jacob had never worked a day in his life. Compared to this kid, he hadn't.

"Split the younger kids up—have them do one thing while we do something else," Corson had told Jacob because he'd no idea what to do except to give them a touch on the shoulder, a bit of help—a nudge forward. Danny was older than any of them by ten years, no longer a kid at all, but he took to numbers right away. When he paid attention, he tackled one math problem after another. Not even Donna thought Danny could make something of himself, but she was wrong. Danny was smarter than most people. He'd just never had a chance.

When the sun fell, Jacob continued to Rachel's house and built a fire in the stove. He pumped water into the kettle and lit one of the kerosene lamps. When he could see the soot-stained walls but not the dooryard out the window, he snuffed the wick and sat at the table facing the field.

Several hours later something came out of the woods—the misfiring cylinder of Phil's truck. The one headlight swam across a warped windowpane, over the mullion, into the next pane, and Jacob thought: I can wipe everything clean and begin again, as his mother had by taking them to Arizona, with her job for church services, with Jesus. He'd tried to do so coming here; no reason he couldn't do so again. All he had to do was leave.

The truck inched forward, and he wondered if she could see him behind the glass. She parked in front of the house and stepped out of the cab carrying her drysuit. When she reached the kitchen, she brushed by him, trailing bottom muck and brine. He lit the lamp, and a moment later she came out of the backroom in dry overalls, sweater, and wool socks. Underneath, he knew, she wore nothing, her arms and legs strong as a man's.

The gray edges of her bangs turned inward. She'd been underwater and had, in changing her clothes, hardened her face. When she reached behind her head to tie a ponytail, he spotted the now familiar tattoo of a propeller on the inside of her forearm. The outline of a cleft appeared in her chin. Green eyes clear as brook ice—the same green as an old shawl from India that Donna kept in a trunk. When they were young, Rachel would wrap the shawl around her neck.

"You say hello to Corson?" he asked.

"Right when I landed."

Rather than reach for her, which was what he wanted to do, he spoke. "Danny killed Gus's sheep."

"*Danny*," Rachel said, raising her eyebrows. "My mother's dog." Not a boy, not a man. A dog. Jacob wanted to ask how his own father had felt before drowning himself in the harbor two years ago. Surely a dog was the envy of his father on that day. "What?" she said. "Why are you looking at me like that?"

He opened his mouth. Instead of cutting them loose from each other, he made the kind of mistake he'd kept himself from making until now.

"I don't know where you're really going tomorrow," he said. "Or what you're doing."

She stepped forward until she stood inches away. "The boat's taking me down to Muscongus for three weeks. I'll be on the bottom, crawling in the friggin' muck."

Everything he'd hoped to avoid burned in her face. But for the flecks of green, her eyes might've belonged to his ex-wife Michelle, who'd once said to him that when he looked at other people, he only saw versions of himself. When he first came back to the island, he had thought that if he could make things work here—if he built enough of a life out here, furrowed enough of a wake—then he and Rachel might stay together, Donna might keep her store. And at first, he thought his efforts with Danny would prove he could make it work.

Rachel sighed and sat on a chair. Her hands rested on her knees. "Has my mother shown you the accounts? The store's been losing money since long before you got here. The last two years've been so bad she's in the hole to Percy's for six months. Didn't know that, did you?"

He didn't see how Donna would ever catch up on six months' debt to her supplier selling bags of flour at just over cost.

"And she buys the books for the school out of her own pocket.

Didn't know that, either? The money that comes from the state doesn't even cover your whole salary."

He shook his head.

"The island used to supplement the teacher's salary, but for the last several years most people aren't kicking in any money. Now my mother does it herself. And what do you think the state will say if they find out you're a surveyor and not a teacher?"

"I never said I was a teacher," he said.

"When you came back," she said, "I thought you were going to help me get us *out* of here." As she spoke to the floor, her voice broke, a sound he hadn't heard since they were kids.

"That's not what I said. I took the teaching job to stay."

"It's been fun playing house all summer while you talked about what you remembered and all your great plans for fixing things. But—*Jesus*, Jacob—I thought you would see what's in front of your face. We can't *live* out here. Not much longer. There's no future. We have to go, and not for a couple weeks to make a few dollars. We have to move across, and I need your help making Corson and my mother see. Instead, you've doubled down on their damned fantasies. Don't look at me that way. I've been telling you all summer. You just don't listen."

"If you wanted to leave so badly, why haven't you just gone?" he said. Before he even started the sentence, he knew the answer. Rachel widened her eyes at him. She had Corson, her mother, and father. None of them would agree to move to the mainland if they could help it, and they couldn't make it here without Rachel. Not for long anyway. She was loyal to them above all else.

"And what you've done with Danny—instead of dealing with the real problem of how the hell we're gonna keep living out here—or what we're gonna do if we can't—you've got my mother all haired up over Danny being in the school. Why would you let that guy into the school? You've got the whole

thing turned upside down. You say all you want to do is help—
Danny, my mother, Corson, even me—but really you're just
pissed off. I don't know why you should be. You're the one who
came back here and landed on *us*. I guess it's your father. You
blame us for your father."

Ever since he'd come back to the island, Jacob had not been
able to picture his father's face. Only his hands, the backs
cracked in a checkerboard pattern. Thumbs hooked and cal-
lused. As a kid in Arizona, his mother constantly reminded him
not to become like his father. If Jacob came home late or got up
late, if he drank one beer, if he sat at the sofa for more than a
few minutes, his mother said he was becoming like his father.
For months after he and his mother first landed in Arizona, he
saw his father everywhere: coming out of the Circle K, walking
through the grocery store parking lot or down Congress Street,
waiting across the street from the school. He often woke in the
middle of the night in the small apartment he and his mother
shared on the far west side of town and convinced himself that
his father padded across the carpet in bare feet in the next room.
Jacob had spent his life chased by his father—not by the man
himself. He hadn't spoken to his father since he was thirteen,
but a person lived in the orbit of what they feared.

"Maybe it's my fault," Rachel said. "I thought when I saw you,
that you'd been living out in the world—I don't know. But Corson's mad for the ground you walk on. Same with my mother."
Rachel cast her hand in the direction of the harbor. "Corson's
got no father, now you show up—what's going to happen when
you leave, too? What's that going to do to them?"

"I'm the one who's talking about wanting to stay."

"The ones who talk about never leaving are the first to go."
Rachel widened her eyes and stepped around him to climb the
stairs.

She was right. He'd only made a mess here. Letting Danny come to the school. And the boy, Corson, he wasn't the boy's father—never would be—and someday Corson would wake with nothing but resentment for Jacob because Jacob'd promised more than he could deliver. And what if Rachel stopped running from him and agreed to stay here with him to raise Corson together? What would he do then?

He stood in the kitchen listening to the thunder of the gathering storm over his head: heels pounding back and forth, doors slamming, trunks clattering. By the time he reached the top step, she'd pushed her clothes onto the bed, packing to go in the morning. He needed her to keep them rooted here, while she needed him to take her away. If they left, he might not want her, and if they stayed, she didn't want him. He sat at the end of the bed.

"Shortly after my stepdaughter Sierra turned four," Jacob said, "I came back from a three-month job in Alaska to find the condo empty, all traces of my wife Michelle and Sierra gone."

Rachel sat next to him on the bed. "Your wife? Your stepdaughter? You're only telling me about them now?"

Jacob recognized the current in his voice, the way he climbed up to the end of the sentence—trying to convince her to keep listening by telling her the very things about himself he didn't want her to know.

"Then a few years later Michelle called and said she wanted to move to Vancouver with her new husband. I asked her not to go even though I had no right to. I'd never apologized for job extensions abroad, women I went off with rather than coming back to Tucson, missed flights, stupid decisions. And she told me that I'd spent no more than four weekends with Sierra in the last two years since we'd split."

When, on his last visit with Sierra, Jacob asked her what she thought about moving to Vancouver, she shrugged, and her tongue darted out to lick the ice cream before the edges melted over the cone. She glanced down the street where her mother had disappeared minutes before.

He tried to picture Sierra: dark hair, brown eyes, her chin a little nob she once rested against his chest when she was still in diapers. She was fading in his mind. No matter what he said or did, Sierra would never come here. She wouldn't understand about Danny, she'd never met Jacob's father, had never even heard the man's name spoken, had never met Rachel or Donna or Gus or Corson. The two of them, Sierra and Corson, would never meet. He would never be able to fix it all.

"They went to Vancouver, and I came here," Jacob said.

Rachel sighed and shook her head. "That's the trouble, isn't it?" she said. "We don't know anything about you."

Jacob said he remembered standing outside this very house when he was twelve and Rachel lived here with her parents. "The window in the eaves was dark," he said, "and when I didn't see you, I went down to the harbor and then the store, and that's where you were, lying on the floor with a lamp reading a book."

"I don't remember that at all," Rachel said, sounding tired.

"You told me, 'I think I want to live at the South Pole.'"

She laughed. "That's what I said?"

He'd talked too much and said too little since he'd come back, and now the smallest fragments of truth felt like scabbed-over memories and useless ploys.

She reached for his hand and clamped it between her rough palms. He didn't know what he wanted her to say, but he was disappointed by her silence.

When she closed her eyes, he did too, and in the darkness, they slipped off the bed onto her still damp laundry. Her thighs warm in the cold as they pulled free of their clothes. She scrambled onto him and gripped his arms and dug her thumbs into his biceps.

In the morning when he woke, the house was empty.

Mango
1974

WHILE CORSON stocked the shelves at his grandmother's store after school, he kept an eye on the island harbor. Someday he was going to leave the island, at least for a short time, and cross the thirty miles to the Main. He'd been to Dennis, directly across, and to Bangor, a couple miles inland. He'd also been to Manan, just another island. He had to wait to travel farther, his grandmother told him, and while he waited, he watched to see who might pull into the harbor.

On the last Monday in May, the *Sunbeam,* an old seiner converted to the church boat, muckled to the island wharf. More than a day late, it wouldn't do much good now; no one would kneel the doss midweek. The *Sunbeam* stopped at the island once every two months so the minister could sing his song, as his grandmother once said. That part offered nothing to look forward to. When the *Sunbeam* came on time, Corson would have to spend an hour sitting on a hard plank pew, down a well of boredom, as the minister raised and lowered them through the morning light.

His grandfather stood on deck gamming with the minister and his old friend, the captain. Corson ran down to join them and climbed onto the deck and bowsprit to lean on the front stay. With his grandfather, he could get away with things that his mother and his grandmother would never let him do. He stepped back onto the deck just as the minister was saying they would have to set sail again that afternoon to keep to their schedule of services at the other islands.

"Your grandfather tells me there's a concert today," the minister said. "It's too bad I won't be here."

With his left hand hidden behind his back, the minister kept staring at Corson. He couldn't stand the minister, but he loved his boat. It was exactly the kind of boat—beamy, 55 feet on the waterline—that he and his grandfather needed. For a couple of years, Corson had pushed a plan for he and his grandfather to take tourists from the Main out to see the puffins on Machias Seal Rock or out to see the Mistake Island Light off Jonesport.

"I have a surprise for you." The minister's hand swung around and presented what looked like an oversized green egg.

"Go ahead, take it."

Corson wrapped his hands around the hard surface, which didn't feel like an egg at all despite the oval shape. Cold as a stone, its skin thick, like the flank of a fish—something from the ocean, but not their ocean.

"It's yours," the minister said. "From California, where someone put it on a truck the size of this boat. The truck drove for days and days across the country until it arrived in your hands." He smiled proudly as if he'd driven the truck himself. "California's that way," he said, pointing west.

"I know," Corson said, and the minister frowned.

"Smarter than he looks," his grandfather said.

Cradling the green egg, careful not to drop it, Corson lowered himself onto the wharf and ran toward his mother's house. When he reached the edge of the field, he saw his mother chopping wood beside the house.

"The minister gave it to me," he said and held it out to her. She picked up the egg one-handed and tossed it above her head. It fell into her open palm but didn't break.

"A mango," she said. The word itself made his lips twist.

She took out her pocketknife, cut an incision, and pulled back the green skin to reveal yellow flesh. She carved out a piece for him and a piece for herself. Corson put his in his mouth. The sweet sting made his eyes water. She cut two more pieces, and they ate them in the shadows of the spruce bows.

Corson closed his eyes and pictured himself in Valparaiso, standing high on the hill above the Pacific. He'd look over the city, the tall church steeples, and the children in colored dresses and shirts, the palm trees. A person would never be the same after visiting a city like Valparaiso. A person would no longer be small.

He and his mother walked toward Boom Beach. She almost never took a break from working, but she seemed in a mood to do so now. When the ocean came into view, she stopped. The low sky had begun to grease. A flock of shearwaters glided over the gray-green water. The birds shrank toward the horizon. Corson had seen shearwaters, more times than he could count. So had she, yet she pointed.

Hunting
1989

HENRY PINKHAM rose before dawn on Sunday, descended the stairs to the basement of his house in East Machias, and looked over the small collection of guns he'd picked up over the years. Mostly hunting rifles, some for birds, some for deer or moose, and one pistol—his father's Colt 1911A1, the closest thing to a work of art he'd ever held in his hand. He planned to meet up with Steve Blizman to hunt down by the point. Steve said he knew the landowner and had permission, but Henry's best guess was that Steve was full of shit.

The land was owned by some guy from New Jersey, so nothing would come of it if Steve was lying. Steve was a man of small mind and even smaller spirit, whose real reason for asking Henry to hunt this morning was to ask for a job. Henry was married to Steve's sister, Angie, so he often found himself standing around nursing a beer while giving Steve advice, which Steve never took. Steve wasn't an idiot. People mistook the kind of fear that tensed every muscle in his body down to his toes for stupidity. Steve was chickenshit; the why of it hardly mattered. This didn't make Henry like him, but it did explain a lot. Henry's father Gus had always said he had survived Vietnam by developing an instinct for who was chickenshit down to their toenails and who wasn't. Truly chickenshit people were fucking unreliable.

Henry had told Angie he would talk to Steve about a job. Angie could manage the lumberyard where she worked, raise their two sons, and look after every weak link in her vast extended family, all in her sleep. She was the opposite of Steve. Her other brother, Richard, also had his shit together. The mystery of genetics. Sometimes Henry had an opening on his crew, but at the moment he had a group of guys he liked, no drunks or halfwits among them. They showed up at the job site, everyone knew what needed to be done, and they went to it. Since leaving the island where he'd grown up, when he was barely into his twenties, he'd managed to pull out of the fishing and smuggling business for good and set up just the right situation. He'd apprenticed with John Crosby and established a reputation among the summer people and the various subs who all protected their turf in the same way lobstermen like his father had protected their grounds. He hadn't worked all these years to get things where he wanted them just to invite a thirty-five-year-old child to ruin everything. Nevertheless, he had to tell Steve something or else Angie would crawl down his throat.

At the bend in the shore road, Henry found Steve standing next to his rebuilt F150 smoking a Kool in full camo with his father's 7.62 National Match M-14 slung barrel down over his shoulder. On the outside, Steve was more or less a fatter—and shorter—version of his father, who had been a scout sniper up near the DMZ where Henry's uncle had died his first month in country. Essentially a Vietnam-era sniper rifle, the National Match was a beautiful weapon that Steve's father had kept in perfect shape before he died of lung cancer. A good caliber for deer, better than the 5.56 Henry had grabbed this morning. The weight of the 14 at eleven pounds would be too much for Steve in no time, and the kick would knock him on his ass if he did try to fire it.

As Henry walked up to him, Steve lit a second cigarette from the first. Two white converse high tops stuck out from under his fatigues.

"Let's go," Henry said and hoofed toward the woods. Steve would start jawing before too long. Henry had to save his energy and tolerance and savor the quiet while it lasted. He didn't expect to see anything they'd want to shoot. Thus the 5.56 Ruger he'd picked this morning because it was less to carry. He'd always wanted to walk the point, maybe because he didn't like the idea of someone else—someone from New Jersey—owning such beautiful land and keeping him out.

What little money Steve made came from clamming and painting houses in the summer. Then he did things like buy a ten-year-old F150 only to have the engine seize a week later. Steve wanted good things for his life but didn't know how to get them. Being a fuck up was part of his bad luck. That was the best way to see the situation. It was getting harder to find a clamming license now with the lottery, so Steve was probably screwed unless Henry hired him.

They stumbled through the new growth pine forest, a replica of the giant forest overhead. The green tips of the small trees hovered several feet above the ground and a fifty-foot canopy blocked the light from filtering down. The more Steve breathed in his ear, the faster Henry walked. He smelled the loam under his feet, the sweet pine, and the salt from the bay only half a mile east.

"I gotta rest," Steve said and slumped against one of the trees. The M-14 dropped into the dirt and Steve's legs splayed out in front. One of the few things Henry's father had said about his own time in the war was that in his job, in small-group patrols near the DMZ, they never put down their weapons—not to eat, piss, shit or sleep. Never. His father had died of cancer within a few years of Steve's father. This thought softened Henry a bit, while the sight of the tarnished barrel lying in the dirt hardened him.

"You should take care of that rifle," Henry said. After Steve's father died, Henry offered to buy it from Steve, but Steve refused.

"I take care of it," Steve said and propped it against the tree. Steve's lower lip stuck out as he pulled in his chin and looked at the ground. The strange thing was that Steve believed what came out of his mouth. He had no idea why the rifle looked like shit, no idea why he had no money, no wife, and a barely functioning car. From their many conversations, Henry had gleaned that Steve thought the world was always screwing him over. He was the kind of person who wanted to tell someone, as if it was a new piece of information, that life wasn't fair. It was clear that he thought of himself as a real American hero for keeping his fucking mouth shut about the shit he'd had to endure—a mother who'd drank too much, a father who'd probably smacked her around, Cheetos on a plate for supper five nights a week, a brother who'd skedaddled to Alaska before Steve turned twelve and come back with a pocket full of money, then his old man had dropped dead before Steve had the chance to impress him.

"And anyway," Steve said, "the gun is my business. It's my gun."

Steve picked up the gun and cradled it in his arms, and Henry thought of his own father cradling his rifle as he ate food from a can in the central highlands. In his final days, Henry's father refused the hospital, refused medication, except for whiskey. He lay in bed at home and stared at the ceiling as his eyes burned. Angie nursed the old man. Otherwise, he would've been left to rot in his own filth. It was all Henry could do to enter the room once in a while and stand there. For two whole days at the end his father moaned as if someone were pulling rusty nails out of his stomach. Henry's mother and sister had died in a fire on the island when he was young. With his father gone, that was it. Henry was the only one left who remembered living out where the mainland was nothing but a distant, gray line.

Henry rose to his feet and kept walking toward the ocean. In addition to Steve's heavy breathing, Henry could hear Steve's boots crunching over branches and leaves. Near the shore, a doe bounded across their sightline and took off toward the bay. Henry didn't think to raise his gun as the doe turned her head and bolted lightly forward, the bottom half of her long legs swallowed by the new growth pines and her body floating across the sparkle of the ocean in the background. She seemed to glide across the water on her knees. Steve stumbled through the woods after her, tripping over fallen logs and the three-foot-wide sink holes created when rotten trees uprooted. Henry followed, in no particular rush. The doe reached the rocky shore and continued into the water without hesitation. The bay was cold, and the waves and the wind blew against the direction she had chosen, directly out to sea.

By the time Henry reached the edge of the water, he felt exhausted even though he had barely exerted himself. With Steve wheezing and coughing next to him, Henry raised his rifle and aimed at the doe, whose margin of escape had only widened by fifty yards. Closing one eye and steadying himself, he exhaled and prepared to squeeze the trigger. For some reason, he didn't. The doe churned through the blue-gray chop at a steady pace. She was headed toward the distant island, a mere smudge on a clear day like this, where Henry had grown up.

Steve fired and missed. His bolt jammed, probably because he never cleaned the mechanism. Henry set his own rifle down, grabbed Steve's M-14, and cleared the jam. The whole rifle needed to be disassembled, cleaned, oiled, and put back together. The word he was looking for was "careless." He had no patience for careless people. Careless people got what they deserved.

He raised the barrel and settled the butt against his shoulder. The rifle was heavy but perfectly balanced. He followed the back of the doe's head plowing through the water. He didn't want to fire without sighting in. He laid the M-14 against a piece of drift-wood and raised his own rifle again. The sea was clear, bright, and clean all the way to the distant islands. The back of the doe's head appeared in the scope. Brown fur, two ears pulled back. He relaxed his shoulders, exhaled, and squeezed. The doe's head went under. There had only been the top of her head to aim at, and now there was no sign that she had been there at all.

In the North
1980

AFTER JACOB'S BUS left Carleton, he fell asleep and didn't wake until he arrived in Portland. There he changed buses and continued to the Boston airport where he waited in line at the counter to check his baggage.

Sitting in back of the plane, he felt the wind buffet the tail fin as the engines strained to push them into the sky. Years ago, when he came home to find Michelle and Sierra gone, the ground vanished beneath him, and he felt a terrifying relief. Now he felt the same relief. He'd launched into orbit once more.

Though he'd told Corson he'd come back soon, he already felt too far away to ever return. The island had shattered in his thoughts. Unable to picture the spruce and granite except in fragments, he thought of Corson looking up every time a plane flew over. He'd never told him about his stepdaughter, Sierra. He'd always planned to tell him; now he'd waited too long and his omission had become a lie and the lie had hardened into a wall between them.

He fell asleep and didn't wake until the wheels touched down in Denver. More waiting in the same kind of chairs facing a tarmac, this time with distant mountains rising into the sky. Then he flew on a smaller plane to Idaho Falls, a smaller airport.

Again in the air, in a plane with two props that bounced through the air currents and set him down past dark in Alberta. The dry, frigid air stuck to the roof of his mouth, stung his eyes, pinched his sinuses. He pulled his face into his collar as he climbed into a cab and directed the driver to the cheap motel next to the airport where he'd stayed before. As preparation for where he was headed, he didn't adjust the thermostat on the wall. Closing his eyes, he crawled under the covers. The falling snow ticked against the window, and out on the road, a plow scraped toward the airport. If the weather didn't let up, his flight would be canceled the next day.

The last time he worked in Alberta he was on the tundra when, halfway into the job, a helicopter came for him in the middle of the day. There was a phone call at the basecamp. On the flight, caribou swam like schools of fish across the land. At the Quonset hut, the pilot cut the engine, and he heard his mother telling him his father had drowned. The police in Maine somehow found her in Arizona and told her the news. Turned out they were still married. After the phone call, he flew back to the outpost and wandered on the tundra by himself. Lay down in a crevice in the pale night. Part of him was still there, with his hands crossed over his chest.

Jacob reached his arm out from under the covers and lifted the phone next to the bed. He remembered Sierra and Michelle's old number in Tucson, but he had to pull Donna's new number in Carleton out of his pocket. Before he headed north, he had to tell them he was coming back.

The ringer buzzed six times. Finally, Corson picked up, and he sighed with relief.

"You're there," he said.

"Where else would we be?" Corson said flatly.

"I don't know. I wanted to talk to someone before I headed

north. I don't want to go." His own voice sounded so young he
looked at the receiver as if it were playing some trick on him.

"You said you had to go. You said you had no choice."

"Yes," he said, though now he wasn't sure. He hadn't even
tried to find surveying work close to Carleton. He didn't want to
say that he feared he wouldn't return. Now that he'd given up on
Rachel, he couldn't be sure what would happen after this job. It
was Rachel's son and mother he really cared about now, but that
might not be enough to draw him back.

"But you'll be back soon," Corson said.

"Yes, I will." Hearing himself say the words, he felt pulled
toward Corson and Donna. Corson said that the truck was act-
ing up again. Jacob said he'd send them some money.

"Are you going to see the Atacama Giant?" Corson asked.

Not long after he came back to the island, he told Corson
about the 390-foot-tall geoglyph carved into the side of a mountain in the Atacama Desert in Chile, the driest place on earth.
Thousands of years ago, the people there spent decades carving
this giant so it could ask the moon for rain. Corson had said
he couldn't picture it. Riverbeds hadn't seen water for 120,000
years. But they had found copper, and that's why Jacob had gone
there.

"No, not this time. I'm in Alberta, remember," he said.

"When're you coming back?"

He'd told Corson many times, six weeks, but now the company had asked for twelve weeks.

"Six weeks," he lied because he didn't want to upset Corson
and because he was used to calling home in the middle of the
night from distant hotel rooms to make promises he wouldn't
keep. First to Michelle, then to Sierra, now to Corson.

"Soon," Jacob said.

"But you're going to come back?"

"Yes," he said, even though images of Carleton, no more home to him than to Corson, wouldn't come to mind.

"You know where we are," Corson told him, and they both said goodbye for now.

He fell fast into a dark, soundless sleep, and in the morning, he woke to the ache of missing them—Corson, Sierra, Rachel, Michelle, Donna, Phil, even Danny—and the fear that he'd always chase after them and never catch up.

The weak light split the curtains. Without thinking, he lifted the phone again and called Carleton so he could make his promise of returning sound more convincing. The phone rang and rang, but no one answered, and he had to hurry to the airport.

Soon he would arrive in the north. The long days outside, and among the few people no one he knew. The dead sky indistinguishable from the frozen land. As the plane lifted over the rolling earth, he gazed out the window and tried to picture the faces of the people he couldn't live without. Forests thick with fallen snow stretched as far as he could see.

Danny's Story
1980

S HE WAS the one who got at him, right inside his head, walk-ing around in his skin. Sarah, his cousin Sarah.

After school, walking down by the harbor, Danny passed her the brown bottle he hid in the stone foundation of Donna's store.

Then she was gone, sent off island by her father to stay with her mother's people on Manan, closer to the mainland. May as well have been halfway across the world.

What he did next was kill all his uncle Gus's sheep with that metal bar he'd found in the woods. Full moon. Blood like oil. No sooner had he dragged the last brained sheep down to the har-bor for his uncle to find in the morning than he started to think about what his uncle would do. Uncle Gus. Gus Pinkham. Kin to everyone, kin to no one, the King Gus Pinkham.

Danny was born on this island to a father who'd never set foot there and a mother who left before he turned six. Didn't matter. Sure as Gus, he was a Pinkham by his mother and by his father a nothing, an unknown, a nobody whose name had never even been spoken. Who cared what all about parents? He could walk into whatever house he wanted to on the island, eat right off the table. He was a Pinkham, same as Sarah. Everyone a cousin, or close to, and he'd talk to whatever person he wanted to, sleep where he wanted to. His uncle couldn't tell him.

The morning after he killed the sheep, Danny heard his uncle Gus yelling his name across the harbor. Danny was hiding on the platform he'd built in the trees. Cupping his hands around his mouth and yelling a second time, his uncle turned in a circle with his hand shading his eyes and passed right over him because Danny was not there. That was his secret. His uncle aimed his fat face at the other end of the harbor, but Danny was not there, either. Not in his shack by the water, not under the store where Danny sometimes slept, not at Donna's house, not under the old boat hauled above the water line at the flake yard. Not in the schoolhouse where Danny kept his desk neat and his pencil sharp. Not anywhere on the island of Outermark where they lived, the sorry rock not less than thirty miles across the water from the State of Maine. Not there, either, not anywhere. The sum of where Danny was not > where Danny was. His uncle had his boat, had his house, had his daughter Sarah—he was *King*—but he did not have math. A man who had math had everything. The island teacher Jacob told him so.

As his uncle stood staring at his dead sheep, Danny raised the good lens of the old binoculars to his right eye and looked down on him. With his other hand, Danny picked up the rusty pistol he'd found behind the Grange and aimed it at his head. Boom. Gus < Gus. Fucker. His uncle lifted his head, but Danny didn't try to hide because not even the King could see him. Gus rested his hands on his hips. What did he know? Made King by the crawlers, Donna always said. No more than a bug himself. Thought he owned Sarah, but he couldn't keep her over to Manan forever. She'd come back. Simple math: Danny would be here.

Then his uncle jerked his head in Danny's direction, and Danny sank to the platform and held his breath. No shouting, no growling, no boots crunching over the rocks, no breaking branches. Nothing but the Motion Ledges gong measuring the length of the swells, the short and the long. Danny looked up through the branches. Cold stung his cheek, and he touched his face with his fingers. Another sting on his forehead and another on his chin. A few flakes tumbling between the boughs melted against his arm, his knuckles, caught in his eyelashes and washed into his vision. He remembered the cold day his mother came back to the island for a visit—the one time Danny remembered seeing her. Shelves of snow piled up along the granite shore. The wind had stopped blowing, the sun turned to ice. Beyond the breakwater, steam rose off the ocean and curled in the air. Danny stood on the wharf as she boarded a boat to leave. He closed his eyes and the image of her appeared—her black hair thick as bayberry and eyes gray as beach clay.

"Danny!" His name split the air. His uncle. "Danny, I know you're out there!"

Just inside the tree-line, only a hundred feet away, his uncle rooted around in the bushes. The bald spot on top of his head shone like a pale egg. Danny lifted the rusty pistol, aimed at his uncle's head, and pulled the trigger. No sound, not even a click. Danny gripped the barrel and held it high. All he had to do was hit the egg and crack the shell and Gus would pour onto the ground.

"Danny!"

As Danny lay back, his uncle's voice spread through the tree-tops and rose like a stain into the sky.

———

Sarah came back, as Danny knew she would, just in time for the dance at the Grange. Against her father's orders, she'd gotten a ride to the island from one of her cousins on Manan, and by the time she arrived in front of the Grange, she was already drunk. Danny was too. He found her on the steps of the Grange trying to say his name, and they were there, too, the teacher Jacob and Sarah's brother and Donna, they wouldn't let him talk to her. They hauled her away to her father's house.

What happened next was that Danny smashed a couple chairs. It wasn't him doing it. He was watching himself do it, like watching a storm rage. He wanted the storm to stop, he even wished Sarah would go back to Manan forever. When he got himself outside in the dark, he took a deep breath of the cool air and saw the treetops waving and the silhouette of the Grange's gable cutting into the sky. In the other direction, the moon traced a trail running southwest across the sea. The silence wouldn't last long, Danny didn't think. People liked to dance.

Minus the twenty steps he'd already taken, he'd two thousand four hundred and three steps left to the schoolhouse. You had to count or you didn't really know anything.

Through the woods, thirty inches to a step. In the field, a trick of the moon Danny knew too well; the trees and the school seemed stretched tall and thin while the light flowed across the field like a rip current. He stepped under the eaves of the schoolhouse and hid in the shadow. Two thousand six hundred steps to the store from where he stood; and from the store, fifty-three steps to his shack on the harbor where he'd not go, not tonight. They'd be looking for him there. Want a word about the broken chairs in the Grange. "Now those were nice chairs," Donna'd say.

"I don't hardly think so," he'd want to say but wouldn't, not to Donna. Donna was the one who said what time it was on the island. No more kin to him than the rock under his shack, she'd taken him in when his own uncle had kicked him out. What Donna said was the rock under the soil. The rock that split the sea.

"You had no business doing that," she'd say. Danny knew exactly what she'd say and felt the sting of it.

Before he took another step, he waited for the usual sounds: wind through the grass, rattle of the thumb latch on the school-house door like Nicky Coffin shaking a bag of marbles in his dooryard. Rattle of a sash loose in its frame on the east side of the school. The low branches of the apple trees scratching through the grass, spruce brushing against each other in the woods, waves gulling Boom Beach, the Motion Ledges gong.

Listen for the sound of their steps: Donna, heels pointed out; Uncle Gus, belly dragging forward, plowing; Jacob, never fast, stepping over the middle of his foot. Each had a sound in the dark. A number. Jacob a four. He walked, he talked, he thought, he breathed. Every fourth breath ran deeper, every four minutes he checked the window. Donna a three—one-two-three, one-two-three. Sarah—one, one, one....

No one had followed him, so Danny stepped thirty inches to the northwest on a heading, jogging it, for Machias Seal Light. They would—his uncle, Henry, even Donna—say Danny'd a habit of turtling, didn't want his own boat except a punky clincher with a donkey engine. No sir! Easy to forget that Sarah wouldn't touch him unless he had his own boat. Forty-plus, high sheer, Cat diesel, Hydro-Slave, the works. Set you back.

When he was young, all the older shits had sixteen-footers with outdrives while all their fathers had real boats you'd see on the outside. Wanted to get his own boat, get out there, like everyone else. Even when the cold shut down. Danny'd get up on thirties like the King, not much to it. Lengthen out, put the warps on 'em. At sixteen Danny fixed an old punt he'd found on the beach. Saved some money from digging clams and other things, bought a shitty outdrive with money Donna'd given him and begged old traps from his uncle. Couldn't make any money but wasn't caught astern by any fault of his own. Nobody tells you shit if it costs them more than it comes to. They'll give you little small hints. Nobody wants to cut their own throat. Nobody wants you to fish around them unless you stick to the mud. Figure everything by yourself. And in the end, you had to have your own boat, Danny knew that. No punt, no skiff, no dory. A real boat. The works.

Danny'd talked to Sarah about having his own boat someday, forty feet, a new Repco, though he could see right away she didn't believe he'd ever have one of the new glass boats. Big money. She said she didn't care about boats, but everyone cared about boats.

If Danny had a boat, his uncle would have to give up space on the wharf and grounds off the Motions. Danny was a Pinkham, same as Henry and Sarah, and if Sarah agreed to marry him, his uncle couldn't say no. Danny was older than her by ten years but a student in the school again. The teacher Jacob had said: to reach your goal you had to say yes to some things and no to others. You had to do things you didn't want to do or feel like doing. You had to have a plan and follow that plan. Danny'd been following the plan until Gus took Sarah to Manan. Then Danny took a few nips, only a few, of what he left under the store. Another bottle in the tree in the woods, and soon he was walking over by the sheep. Their stupid black eyes. They dodged him as if there was something wrong with him. It seemed like a long time ago, and Danny was a different person when he killed those sheep than he was now—woke in the morning and saw them floating in the harbor—even though it was only a few days past.

He'd been on the outside, though Gus and the rest would say he hadn't. April month, May month, first time five years ago, and he knew the marks and deeps, learned it on Pat Petingale's rig. Flossie's brother, out of Manan—kin to himself. His uncle Gus took him to Manan when Danny turned sixteen and handed him off to Pat. Wanted shut of his sister's kid. First time with Pat, they cruised out beyond the basin. That boat could take more than you could. Scare you to death before it hurt you. Pat a fair man, unlike the other Petingales. A full share of a good trip would put planks on the frame of a new boat. A second bought the diesel. Could've gone that way, but they motored around changing the water. Ran into tropical birds on the outside, blown off course. Pulled up the traps and seen all these fish, really colorful and exotic, come off the Stream from the south. Sculpin, skates. One night—never been in weather that bad—Danny found three feet of water and everything floating in the forward cabin. Automatic pumps running, but now the pumps were losing. "Take the wheel, Danny," Pat said, so Danny took the wheel. Couldn't even see the bow of the boat, so much water rolled over the top. Just the compass showed. "Hold this heading," Pat yelled. Danny'd never steered a boat that big. Waves hit so hard the plywood under the fiberglass on the wheelhouse blew out and water rolled over the side. Pat tried to bodge it together, while Danny'd the skitters running down his friggin' leg.

Out there for hours before they made Yarmouth pier, Nova Scotia. Pat said, "Gonna be a few days to put this boat together." Danny found an abandoned car parked in front of a beach. Slept in the car, and Pat took him back to the island the day a jet flew over and a sonic boom broke the sound barrier.

As Danny walked through the woods after breaking the chairs, he had to keep an ear out because they'd be after him. He stood so long leaning against a tree he felt like his arms had become branches and his skin had turned to bark. His heartbeat the only sound that didn't belong, but they were out there: Donna would have something to say, his uncle, too. Their names a tapping rhythm in his head as Danny walked: Donna. Donna Wills. Donna Cushing Wills. Gus. Gus Pinkham. Henry

Pinkham. Henry George Pinkham. Henry George Petingale
Pinkham. They'd want their chairs back. Sarah, too. Sarah.
Sarah Pinkham. Sarah Petingale Pinkham. They'd all be after
telling Sarah how high Danny held the chairs above them—
threatened their lives with their chairs. Sarah had said she liked
the sound of his voice. Danny. Danny Pinkham, her cousin
Danny. Danny Ingersoll Pinkham. Liked his stories about when
her father used to pass out on the wharf on the Main with his
pants around his ankles. He wished Sarah would go away and
not come back for good. It would take forever to forget the smell
of her hair.

When Danny came down the road to the harbor a tall heron
spread its wings, as wide as a punt long, and lifted into the air.
Swells rose over the granite, spruce branches waved. Moonlight
choking off, temperature dropping. Danny couldn't head to his
shack, where they'd all know to look for him. No one bothered
the shed back of the store, used for firewood, and around behind
the firewood a stall the size of a man lying down that'd once
been used for coal. A good spot to hide in the summer when
the firewood ran low. Other places, too, no one knew about: a
couple of boards nailed together twenty feet in a tree over by
Leech Pond, with cans up there, a jug, only good in the summer.
A man could stay in the abandoned Gooch place for some time
before anyone thought to check, or the cab of the rusted Chevy
in the woods behind the Grange.

Under the store, his favorite place this time of year, when the
cold set in. Danny slipped through a gap in the granite slabs and
crawled along the ledge until he lay directly under the cookstove.
Old chunks of Styrofoam under here. Three cans of beans, a can
of fruit, and a jug of water. A jar of Irish, the real thing. With
the ledge sloped, a man could turn and the piss would drain to
the harbor. A man could stay under, warm enough. During the
day feet tapping overhead like talk radio, Donna's rocker rutting

grooves in the floor, and her grandson Corson's stool tap, tap, tapping. Everyone's steps: Vince, oatmeal face, Benny, Phil.

Danny wedged himself close and rested his palm against the rough lumber where he kept some almost-full bottles. He unscrewed the top and tipped it back. Heat spread through his chest and into his limbs. Jacob and Donna out there looking for him in the school, the Grange, the shack on the harbor, Boom Beach, along the wood's trails, all places he was not.

Donna's husband Phil would hire him to get the wood in, Benny too—a few dollars, a few cans from Donna. Danny could make money on the island by handlining, sterning, maybe for Stoven, but he'd never save enough money that way. A man had to move to the Main, and that's why he'd come back to the school. Like Jacob said, *Make yourself useful.* A lot had done the same. Stoven, Gus, Benny Coffin, all came back with enough money to build their own boats. Phil had been in the Merchants and that's how he got the money for his boat.

With no boat, you had nothing but a shack and lucky to have that. Sarah would never lie in his shack, never crawl under the store with him. Said Danny was funny to listen to, liked to bend her elbow with the stuff he bought, wasn't going to let him touch more than her elbow. Not without his own boat. No matter what they told you, no matter what she said, Sarah wouldn't touch him until he'd a boat, because in order to have a table on this rock, you needed a house, and in order to build a house you needed a boat. Needed all those things, or when she looked at you, her eyes saw through to the other side, and you weren't there.

One day as they walked to school up the road from the harbor, Danny showed Sarah a picture of the car he wanted to buy after he had his own boat and had saved enough money. Not a Chevelle but a real car, a Corvette, Danny told her. Red. He might want to see California. Had to keep her attention by saying interesting things. "California," she repeated. "People go waterskiing," Danny said. "You hold a rope tied to a boat and stand on a board and the boat pulls you all over the water while you wave at people." True enough. Danny'd read descriptions in magazines, which Donna brought back from the Main all the time and kept in the store. "Ask if you don't believe me. Donna'll show you," Danny said. She laughed but not meanly. Thought he was funny, said so. "I know about waterskiing," Sarah said. A couple days later, before Gus shipped her over to Manan, they were out in the field and she touched him on the arm. Not by accident, either. She let her fingers stay there above the elbow where the surface of the skin still tingled.

Danny fell asleep with his left hand on the elbow where Sarah had touched him, warm on his Styrofoam bed with the jacket Donna had given him draped on top. The boat Danny wanted would be forty-two feet, not forty. A Novi hull, like those Manan boats, high in the bow, high sheer. All fiberglass, top to bottom. Cat diesel. Hydro-Slave hauler.

He woke later to what sounded like a yell and the rush of water over the bow, but when he sat up, he was not on a boat, not on the outside. On the island, at the harbor, the waves crashing against the breakwater. Late now, dark with his eyes open or closed, no difference, so he left them open. Thirsty, and he had to shit. He lifted the bottle to his lips and drank with his head turned sideways.

To his left, along the foundation wall facing the harbor, dim light flickered in the cracks between the granite slabs and grew brighter until he could see his boots and the adze marks in the beams over his head. He slid across the rock and peered over the harbor. Someone stood on the Pinkham wharf holding a hurricane lamp high. He wound the cap onto the bottle, tucked it into his pocket, scrambled from under the building, and ran along the shore trail toward the Pinkham's house. The light drifted toward the kitchen door, and Danny yelled Sarah's name even though the light could belong to Gus or Sarah's mother, Flossie.

"Sarah!" Danny called and the person stopped, held the lantern high. She didn't run away, and in another three leaps, Danny reached her.

"You can't be here," Sarah whispered. She grabbed his arm. Her breath smelled of hooch but not the stuff Danny'd given her before. He looked down at her hand on his sleeve to make sure it was really hers.

"Someone will see us," she said and tugged him toward the kitchen door. "You have to be quiet. My mother's asleep upstairs." Once inside, she set the lantern on the kitchen table, shut the door behind him, and fell against his shoulder. She swayed, almost knocking him off balance. He'd never been this close to her. He needed to say the right thing. Instead, he pulled the bottle out of his pocket and held it up to her. She took it and turned it upside down into her mouth. The brown liquid in the light. Danny thought she might fall on her face, but she didn't. She lowered the bottle, held it up, handed it back. "Drink!" she commanded in a rough voice.

"Shhh!" Danny said. Flossie might wake. His uncle was just outside in his shack. Danny took the bottle and swallowed until only three fingers remained.

"The fucker!" she said so loudly Danny was sure her mother heard. Then Danny thought she must be talking about him.

"My brother—my father! Both of them." She fell straight to her knees and struggled to rise. When Danny leaned over to help her up, she pulled him down and wrapped her hands around the back of his head. His nose pressed into her neck, his lips against her salty skin. She kissed his cheeks, his forehead. Her tongue slipped over his teeth, and his thoughts tilted. He floated above the house, above the harbor, where no one could touch them.

Something slammed against the top of his head, throwing him against the door. When he opened his eyes, Danny thought he would see his uncle standing over him, but it was Sarah risen to her knees with the heel of her hand still pointing at him like the barrel of a gun.

"Go!" she said, and when Danny didn't speak, she pitched forward and threw up onto the floor. Danny reached her shoulder, but she shoved him against the wall and pushed him outside. Danny didn't realize he was running until he was halfway to the store. Looking over his shoulder, he saw her swaying in the doorway with the lamp on the table behind her. When he took a step toward her, she turned into the kitchen.

Later that night, Danny woke from his spot under the store and saw light flickering between the stones of the foundation. He thought maybe he would see Sarah coming back to find him, but it was her whole house on fire. He was too late by the time he reached her front door. Flames had burst out of her bedroom window and started to climb up the shingles. He ran around back but couldn't get close enough to open the door or any of the windows, so he ran to the only place he could think of and hid in one of his uncle's old boats pulled up on shore. He waited there for the fire to come for him. Was sure it would. They were surrounded by water for miles in every direction, but it wouldn't matter. Hearing a roar, he braced for the heat, flames so hot they would stab like ice, but cold air rushed under the boat and water pooled under his knees. The rain came in sheets with the wind.

He had no idea how long it had been since the fire snuffed out and the woods around Gus's house stopped steaming and smoking. He had to remind himself that he hadn't started the fire because they would think he had. Donna soon found him and she sent him to the Main—for his own good, she said—but he couldn't stay where he didn't know anyone and no one knew him. He made his way back to the island by hitching and steeling a dory, and once there, he hid in the schoolhouse. In the light of day, with hunger lodged like a knife in his gut, he waited as the sun ticked across the sky. No sound but the Motion Ledges gong ringing with the swells, telling him, *Sit down, Danny, sit down, Danny.* He was already sitting and had no intention of standing. The wind through the trees behind the school said the same thing. He hadn't locked the door. No point. The door clattered in the rising wind, a loose pane knocked in the back sash. The bare branches scraping each other in the woods behind the school. When the wind died, the gong sounded louder in the air, twitting. Thinking of Sarah, his eyes squeezed shut, then open, and Danny knew what he saw: not clouds, not sky, not gulls hanging in the air. Nothing but the color white.

He rested his hands on the top of the desk, stared at Sarah's empty chair, and thought of her swaying drunkenly with the kerosene lantern in her kitchen. Half burned, they took her to the Main. Now her desk was no longer hers.

Boot heels scraped along the dirt road and pant cuffs brushed through the grass. Danny didn't have to raise his head to know who it was. His cousin Henry standing in the doorway. His uncle behind him at the edge of the field.

"Stand up, Danny."

Danny didn't stand right away. When he did rise, he did so because with Sarah gone—gone forever—everyone on the island would look right through him. He was no longer there.

Henry let him walk ahead. Henry didn't speak, didn't slow down, didn't speed up, all the way to the harbor. Henry wouldn't even look at him when they reached the store where he opened the woodshed. Pushed from behind, Danny stumbled forward.

Before he could take a seat on the stump where Phil split kin-
dling in the winter, the door shut behind him and the iron latch
clicked. A loose plank behind the woodpile would let him drop
under the store. Hide there for days or slip along the pinch and
crawl up the hill next to his uncle's. Take the trail to the tree
he'd clad in the woods behind Gooch's. A tarpaper roof. No one
knew the spot. But there was no use hiding when you were not
there. No use hiding unless someone waited for you to come
back.

A blade of sunlight cut across the planks and lodged in the
woodpile. The rumble of his uncle's twin Cat diesel rattled in
his chest. Henry swung open the door and stood with his face
angled at the ground, sticking out his lip. Henry, a year older
than him. *No longer a boy.* His uncle had said so. You have nothing if you don't have your own boat.

"Come out here." Henry's voice was soft, like the minister's.
The first time in his whole life his cousin didn't try to sound
bigger than he was.

"I tried to go back for her," Danny said even though he had
stayed hidden under the boat the whole time.

"Come on."

Henry pointed to the end of the wharf where his uncle waited
for them in the boat. One seagull circled the marker pole. No
one had come down to the harbor to see them off. He spotted
Donna sitting on her porch, watching them. Danny climbed
down the ladder first, Henry after. They'd muckled a punt with
no oars to the stern. This was the old way.

Outside the harbor, headed south-southeast, Gus hit the
throttle. The water turned gray. Nothing on all sides except the
foaming wake trailing behind them. Spray from the bow fanned.
As they pushed east of the Jordan Basin, swells stretched out,
wind raked the beam. Even a boat as large as the *Flossie* felt like
driftwood in the Northeast Channel, over Brown's Bank, near

the Gulf Stream, warm water flowing north. Danny had sailed this way with Flossie's brother Pat, what seemed like a thousand years ago. As they pushed toward the Stream, the range grew steep, and for a moment Danny thought he saw one of the old ships with three masts. There was just one mast, though—a dragger riding the crest of a swell and headed northeast away from them.

When Danny closed his eyes and tried to picture Sarah, he could see the outline of her face, her blonde hair, but her cheeks had turned gray. He couldn't see the island. It was as if he hadn't been born there. As if the island didn't exist.

He opened his eyes and saw that the sun had dipped. His uncle throttled down. The hull weighed into the next swell like a hand slipping into a mitten.

Henry pulled the punt in close while his uncle walked to the stern, steady on his feet. Henry rested his hand on Danny's shoulder as if they were old friends. Henry's pupils were so black that Danny felt his own thoughts turning black.

Henry and his uncle lifted him by the arms and lowered him so that his legs dangled above the punt.

"Watch his legs," his uncle said. Danny lifted his legs just before the punt slammed the hull so hard that the punt's garboard cracked. "Now," his uncle said, and both he and Henry set him into the punt. With a flick of his wrist, Henry uncleated the line, and the punt floated free. In seconds Danny'd drifted twenty yards northeast. When Gus throttled up again, the rumble of the engine shook the air. White spray feathered out from the bow as they headed west. They stood with their backs to him. Soon they were stick figures, then there was just the tiny shape of the boat shrinking on the horizon and the sound of the engine like someone's breath in sleep.

The giant swells lifted and lowered him as chop lapped the hull of the punt. At his feet, only planks and a plastic bleach bottle cut in half as a bailer. No oars, no locks. As the swell lifted him again, he stood in the boat, the tallest thing for miles, and searched the mountains of water rolling toward the edge of the sky. He searched over his shoulder in the direction of the island and the mainland, and he searched to the south in the shipping lane. The punt slid into the trough of the next swell and darkness began to close like a fist around him. Soon there was nothing but the sound of the wind and the water slipping under the planks of the punt.

The Blue Heron
1970

Too big for the sky and unfit for the water, a blue heron—long, aquiline beak, a puffed crown, dangling legs and sharp claws, wings unfolding from a lean body and expanding like sails—glides over the island of Outermark and lands in front of the church. The door stands open. Children have been playing here, running up and down the aisle until they grew dizzy and ran home. The blue heron walks inside. His wings drag like coat tails. A ray of orange light filtering through the window freezes in the rising dust.

Janet's Story
2022

I UNDERSTAND THAT the history of a place should include the stories of people who were not born there, but I'm not sure I'm the person you have in mind for your archive. Though I've lived here in Carleton for half my life, I never wanted to move here to begin with and am not sure why I stayed. If you want to speak to someone about this place, I recommend you talk to Corson Wills, the head of the library. Like me, he wasn't born here, but he's from Maine, he knows all the history. Unlike me (I'm liable to tell you things that will exclude this little tale from the annals of regional history), he's a private person. In other words, he's more likely to stare at you until your frontal lobe melts than tell you his favorite flavor of ice cream. I suggest you start by asking about the Dewey Decimal System and move on to something more personal like the library acquisition budget. It'll be good for him. If you try him at his office at the library, he's less likely to close the door on you. Tell him I sent you. He and I worked together for many years. He doesn't like to disappoint an old lady, particularly one of his dearest friends. In fact, go ahead and tell him I called him one of my "dearest friends." He hates talk like that, but it will work.

In terms of how *I* ended up here, I really don't know what to say. I was born in New Jersey. I arrived in a paneled station wagon as long as an aircraft carrier. I don't even live in my own house. My name is on the deed, but I didn't buy the house. My former husband bought it while we were still married. We lived in Connecticut at the time, and he told me over supper that he'd bought a second home for us in Maine while he was there on a business trip. He'd just signed a contract to supply the state corrections system with toilets, so he was flying high, I guess. I was pregnant with our daughter, Bridget. He told me the name of the town and described the house to me. If I didn't like it, he said, we could sell it, but he'd gotten a good deal.

We stayed in the house summers, for a few weeks at a time. Bridget and I went to the beach while he worked. When my husband and I divorced, I needed somewhere to live. He didn't like Maine after all, and I didn't mind it. I also needed money before the divorce was settled, so I found a job working at the front desk of the Patten Free Library, where I met Corson. He had just started high school and only worked a few hours in the afternoon. He had only lived in town for a few years and was younger than my own daughter. He spoke so little, and always in a heavy accent I didn't recognize. I thought maybe he had come from Canada originally, which wasn't far from the truth.

A lot happened during my first years at the library—I had an affair with my boss and spent some days in the hospital that I thought would be my last days on earth. I don't know that Corson and I were that close, really, until later, when his grandmother died. He must've been seventeen then, still in school. I remember he showed up at work the morning after she passed. I found him standing at the threshold of the reading room and noticed right away that there was something different about him. For the first time, he didn't have his lunch clutched under his arm. He always clutched something—bags, apples, books, sweaters. He was a clutcher. This morning his empty hands stuck out to the sides. The skin over his cheeks and forehead was always dry, as if he washed his face with sand. I always worried that he didn't eat enough.

Sandra, the nurse I knew from my stint in the hospital, had called me the night before and told me about his grandmother. "I thought someone should know," Sandra had said. "The boy has no other family here in Carleton." Corson looked after his grandmother all by himself.

I led him into the reading room and sat him down in one of the wing chairs next to a glass-covered model of a clipper ship. Some eager octogenarians had even installed a tiny captain on the model's deck with blond hair and a blue hat. Usually, Corson showed up early to work to read in the magazine room, but he didn't have his book with him today.

"I'm not feeling too well," Corson said. "I might pass out. That's the way it feels, like I might stop breathing." Corson's eyeballs pushed out of his sockets, willing his awful predictions to come true.

"I don't think those things will happen," I said. "Not today."

"I don't want you to call the doctor," he said.

"I won't," I said and got him to lie on the floor.

"Someone will see me down here," Corson moaned.

"It's still early. We haven't opened the doors yet."

Corson clutched his chest and gazed out the portico window above our heads, as if to search for the light that would guide him to a peaceful afterlife. Fortunately, the head of the library, Tony, who liked to arrive before the "sunrise club," had yet to show up.

"My grandmother's dead," Corson said. "Last night."

"I know. I heard."

Corson squeezed his eyes shut as I sat with him, and gradually his breathing subsided.

"You don't have to worry about me," Corson said, and I refrained from saying that someone had to. With a sudden display of determination, Corson pinched his lips together and took up his position at the front desk where he sat upright and rigid, ready to check out people's books. I didn't just worry about the shock of his losing his grandmother. I had started to worry about him six months before when his jaw had slackened, his shoulders had slumped. Even his curly brownish-red hair had seemed to grow brittle.

"I think I should go home," Corson said and leaned his head against the counter. "But I need to talk to Tony."

"No one *has* to talk to Tony, except his wife. Poor woman."

Taking Corson's arm, I led him out the front door and used my keys to lock up.

"What about the library?" Corson asked.

"Fuck the library. Tony will be here soon. He can man the front desk for once."

As we crossed the park, Corson lifted each foot as if it weighed ten pounds. We hadn't traveled more than a hundred yards when he sat down on one of the benches. I joined him. From our position, slightly elevated on a knoll and hidden among half a dozen groomed pines, I watched Tony park his car in his assigned spot and walk along the paved path toward the front doors. Tiny head atop a long narrow body, a few wisps of dirt-colored hair swept over a sweaty eggshell dome. What had I been thinking? Cagey minnow eyes behind the kind of rimless glasses that always looked bent out of shape. Not to mention his grotesquely red lips. The red lips got me every time—like discovering a leach on my thigh.

"Watch this," I said. Tony came to the front door, tugged, and stumbled back. He tugged again, shaded his eyes to look inside, and finally began to rub his head. He returned to the glass door, dropped his shoulders, and started pounding.

"I have usually unlocked the doors by now," I said, and the corners of Corson's mouth curved upwards. "He comes in after the shift starts," I said, "and he leaves before the shift ends, so Herr Tony doesn't need to worry about a little thing like keys."

"His wife would beat him if he came home ten seconds late," Corson said.

"Now I'm going to tell you something you may not want to hear," I said. "I used to have sex with that man after I first moved here."

"I *know* that," Corson said. "You told me a few years back, when you were sick."

One of the things I loved about Corson—he didn't say much, but once he felt comfortable around you, he let himself say whatever he wanted to.

"One day he looked okay to me. He had more hair back then. And he said I reminded him of one of the Brontë sisters. He didn't say which one, which should've been a clue. Probably I was just lonely. Loneliness leads to sex. *In the library. In the middle of the night.* And we always had to use my keys to get in. So I know he leaves his keys at home."

That part I'd never told anyone. Corson shook his head. For a few minutes, Tony paced back and forth in front of the door.

"Grandma said she wanted to be cremated and that I should toss 'whatever was left' of her into the Kennebec River when the time came," Corson said. "I don't know. I called my mother in Alaska and left a message, but she might be out to sea with her husband. There's the church up on Washington Street. Grandma only went there on Easter and Christmas because she said there was nothing on the radio those days."

I knew that Corson's grandmother no more thought of Carleton as home than a captain circumnavigating the globe thought of his ship as his destination. Corson and his grandmother were from a small island thirty miles or more off the Maine coast. I had looked it up on a map at one point—a green dot between Maine and Nova Scotia, smack in the middle of

the Bay of Fundy. Outermark. There was very little information. One short article in the *Bangor Daily* described a fire that
destroyed a house on the island. Shortly afterwards the people
living there, including Corson's family, moved to the mainland.

"I don't know what to do," Corson said. "Grandma liked the
church OK, which reminded her of the church on the island,
but she didn't like the way Jesus was dressed, on the cross. She
didn't like hippies much, and Jesus reminded her of a hippie.
Once she asked the minister if he would play Johnny Cash
during the service instead of the organ music."

The "sunrise club" began to arrive in the parking lot of the
library. Small gray heads hunched over the steering wheels
of oversized cars. A number of those blue USS WHATEVER
hats covering sun-blotched pates. With stunted steps, they
descended on Tony, who scanned the park surrounding the
library while shading his eyes.

"He sees us," Corson said. "You're going to get in trouble."

"It's not your fault," I said, "and no one's in trouble. Makes it
all worth it—my lawsuit with the city. We can do almost anything we want to Tony."

I held both hands in the air and waved.

———

After work, I invited Corson over to my house, where I reheated
the soup I'd made the previous day. I tried to ask him questions
about his grandmother and offered to help him with the details—
the arrangements. There are always details and arrangements.
He barely responded as he sipped from his spoon. I started to
talk about my barn in part because it's a nervous habit I have
when another person doesn't speak. Also, though, I hoped to
distract him from his troubles with my own.

"I feel as if I can't get going on anything until I do something about the barn," I told him, and he looked at me. "I hired a girl who comes to the library. I call her a girl, but she is probably your age. When she came over, I opened the door to the barn, and I thought she would pass out. She couldn't help me at all. She was useless, and I can't blame her. Clothes, furniture, old bikes, books—in piles everywhere. Most of it is Bridget's; I can't throw it out."

"When was the last time your daughter was home?" he asked. The first thing he had said in what felt like a long time.

I told him that a month or so before I had received a letter from Bridget, sandwiched among the bills. It was still a time in which people wrote letters, but it was not a time in which I received many. I hadn't seen her in several years. In the letter she said she wanted to visit and named a date and time when she would arrive by bus in the next town over. I immediately wrote back explaining that I would be happy to pick her up at the airport and pay for the ticket, but I never heard back from her. She didn't have a cell phone or a computer in the camp where she worked, and my letter had to travel all the way to Africa. If she could have taken a Greyhound bus—or even a slow, miserable ship—across the Atlantic, she would have done so.

"When is she supposed to get here?" he asked.

"The day after tomorrow, and I don't know what she might want and what she might not want."

"You should have told me."

"I've been paralyzed by it, completely."

"Can't you call her and ask her what she wants from the stuff, and you could throw the rest out?" Corson asked.

"I can't call her where she is in this border camp. And it's not just her things. It's everything from when I was married, a lot of my parents' things. What if Bridget wants something when she comes back? She won't be able to find it."

"I don't know," Corson said.

"You know what?" I said apropos of nothing, just wanting to change the subject before I felt overwhelmed with anxiety thinking about Bridget. "I was thinking about you the other day and remembered when I was sick how you used to bring food over to my house."

"Grandma liked to cook for people," Corson said.

"It was very thoughtful of you," I said.

Corson shrugged.

"And then I decided that you should go to Bowdoin College. You're going to graduate high school next year. You're smart; you can't waste away in this library for the rest of your life. Working for Tony! We can get you a scholarship."

"No," Corson said firmly. "College would be like high school. Everything smelling like, I don't know, old teeth."

In the newspaper article I had read about the fire on the island where Corson was from, there was no detail about how the fire had started. Only that it arrived in the middle of the night and took the people there off guard. If a rainstorm had not arrived, the entire island would have burned.

"First my grandma couldn't sleep at night," Corson said, "then she wouldn't eat, and then she had trouble walking up the hill from Front Street. She blamed old age, she blamed the mud, then she blamed the fish tea I made. Said it turned. I told her, *your recipe*. When her breath started to sound like someone crumpling a paper bag, I called Doctor Hale. I didn't tell her I had called because she owned her own medical encyclopedia and thought a person shouldn't pay a mechanic for something they could fix themselves."

"I'm sorry," I said.

"Why are you sorry?" Corson looked at me.

"It's just an expression. I mean I'm sorry things were so hard. You should've called me. With your mother on the other side of the country...."

When I asked if he felt better now, Corson didn't answer. He just stared at his hands with the kind of complete concentration he devoted to reading during his lunch hour.

"You had a lot of people on your side," Corson said. His cheeks blushed slightly.

I had no idea what he was talking about.

"With the...thing with Tony."

"The people on one's side in these things can be more trouble than the people against you."

"I was just a kid," Corson said, and I said, "Exactly." I wanted to say, "*Still are!*" He still had more than a year of high school left.

"Listen," I said. "The most amazing thing happened at the library yesterday during your day off. The kind of thing that can make your decade. You know Tony's private bathroom," I said, "and how we always know he's in there because there is a little window above the door, and we can see the light go on."

Corson nodded.

"Well," I said, "the light goes on, and at the front desk, we all raise our eyebrows, because the light only goes on when he needs to stay awhile, you know what I mean, and that only happens at 2 p.m. every day. Tony the 2 p.m. man. But yesterday he goes in at nine, at ten-thirty, and again at eleven-thirty—what did Carol feed him the night before? After his last time, he comes out with a length of toilet paper hanging out of his khakis as long as a fox tail."

Corson smiled.

"But that's not all," I said. "He doesn't realize it's there, and he starts doing his rounds of the library: the Reading, to make sure we've put all the magazines and newspapers back the way he likes them; Children's, to make sure the little rats are not chewing on his books; Computers, to make sure the teenagers are not sticking gum on the keyboards. He does the whole library, and not one person tells him—not one person! At the end of the day, he puts on his coat and goes home with his toilet paper tail. And you know the best part of all," I said, and I let off a little whistle for dramatic effect. "The best part of all—and here I admit I am having to stretch a little, because—but I know this is what happened when he got home. He took off his coat and went into the kitchen to see that wife Carol who's been slaving away for hours to make him dinner. He pats her on the head and tells her it smells good and then when he turns to make himself a nice stiff drink, she sees the toilet paper sticking out of his pants, and she reaches over and snips it right off. She just snips off his tail and drops it in the trash. Doesn't say a word about it, and he doesn't have the slightest idea. He shows up at work the next morning, and he's the only one there who doesn't know he walked around the whole previous day flying a bum paper flag out of his pants. Don't you think that's how it happened?" I asked.

"I do," Corson said, and added that it was the best story he'd heard in a long time. He sat up and took a deep breath.

"Will you come with me to the bus stop when I pick up Bridget?" I asked him. "I don't have anyone to go with me. I don't know why I need someone to go with me, but I do."

"Yes, of course," he said.

"And I want to help you with…with your grandmother."

"I don't know what to do," he said in a whisper. "I don't know what she would want me to do."

"We'll figure it out," I said. At first, I didn't think he had heard me, but then he nodded.

"Right now, why don't you show me what needs to be done in the barn," he said.

"Oh, it can wait," I said. But Corson told me it would be good to take a look.

"I'm afraid to even turn the light on in there."

It was an old barn with a rusted iron latch on a heavy wood

sliding door. I unhooked the latch and pulled the door to the right. I reached around the corner, flipped a switch, and a bare light, hanging from a beam by a wire, cast a glare.

"You see what I mean?" I said. There was one open area filled with piles of boxes, plastic and paper bags, hanging dress bags, dark varnished bureaus and tables and trunks, half-opened boxes of plates, stuffed animals, wooden toys spread around, and a cracked leather saddle. A path through the middle of the barn exposed the worn boards of the floor. I walked halfway to the back wall, turned to a small dress bag, opened the zipper, and pulled out a child's dress.

"This belonged to Bridget, when we lived in Connecticut," I said. I reached into a cardboard box and pulled out sheaves of lined paper covered in long cursive letters. "Her school papers. After the divorce, I ended up with everything. All the furniture—everything she left behind. I don't know where to start. I don't know what to save and what to get rid of."

Kuankan, Guinea, near the border with Liberia—a place I would know nothing about if I hadn't met Hamilton Hartman in an East 33rd Street bar in 1962.

"Tell me this," Hamilton once said, after we had been married several years. "Do you think men are born smarter than women?" I told him no. "Do you think men are more practical than women?" I admitted that sometimes they were. "Ahh, sometimes!" he said, as if I'd made a fatal mistake in the legal defense of my gender. I asked him how he would define intelligence. "Knowing when to be quiet," he told me. He was talking about washing machines again—or toilet valves—against the one rule I had for the house. He had spent the first years of our marriage, when his parents were still alive, talking about the parts for washing machines and toilets his grandfather had introduced to the world. The measure of all intelligence: the H-23L valve. Also, The S-5 and the H-943 and the H-143. The first device described by the inventor as the "detachable fixture with apertures used to manipulate water from its source and keep the bowl clean." The only real "game-changer" in toilet history.

The one rule he had for me in the household (typical Episcopalian move): no crass language. Says the grandson of the H-23L *shit valve*. I had not grown up in a house with any crass behavior, or crass language. I only started swearing after I met Hamilton and had to endure hours of technical discussion about the device used to carry people's feces out of the house and into the underground maze of shit storage. So once in a while I said the word Shit! aloud. Always with exclamation, and a few times in front of his parents before they died. That I may have hastened their end weighed less on my conscience than the feeling that marrying Hamilton Hartman—a rich man—may have put my own parents into an early grave.

The Hartmans, the only Episcopalians I knew who didn't appreciate art. Before the H-23L, which they sometimes referred to (without irony) as the Sloping Suck Valve (if that wasn't crass, I didn't know what was), they had been immigrant plumbers. I was raised as a lover of books and art and couldn't fix a leaky sink. I had not grown up rich, had grown up, in fact, to despise the rich. My parents, both teacher-socialists, had raised me to see wealth as the pure manifestation of culpability. No such thing existed, in their world, as successful rich people. You looked to Martin Luther King Jr., their hero, and the artists and anarchists of Greenwich Village. Bankers, stockbrokers, slumlords, manufactures, all villains. Yet one year out of NYU, floating from one apartment share to another as I filed for a midtown ad agency, I met Harold Hartman, *HH* monogrammed

on his shirt, at an East Side bar. Looking back, I had to see this
moment clearly: he, she. He couldn't take his eyes off me. He
sidled up next to me, waited for me to spot him, and then said in
a low voice, so my friends would not hear, "I noticed from over
there—you're very beautiful."

Not drunk, not smirking. Not a dare. He didn't offer me
a drink (I had been offered plenty of drinks before), and he
didn't ask for anything. I studied his hands. Maybe, if he had
been handsome, I might have turned away—too many handsome boys around then, before they all grew out their hair and
stopped shaving. He had long flicking lashes.

"HH," I said, "buy me a drink," because that's what bold
women in bars said then, though I'd never said it or even heard it
said. I saw when he smiled and still didn't look up at me that this
one's shyness was no ploy. No younger than me, surely, but a boy
with a soft jawline, dimples, and a beach tan. The Santa Claus of
comfort—some weakness in me began to sink toward him.

That week I had filled out an application for teacher's college
(never wanted to see the inside of an office again) and planned
to quit my job. Two of my former roommates from NYU talked
of driving to Mississippi to help people register to vote, and
I had thought of going with them. It was not long before the
James Meredith riots at the University of Mississippi, little
more than a year before the murders of Chaney, Goodman, and
Schwerner in Neshoba County. I, who had studied art and literature and French, knew nothing of Boynton v. Virginia and had
heard only vague reports from my friends of the bold exploits of
the Freedom Riders.

If HH's voice had not trembled so badly as he said that he just
wanted to talk to me, I wouldn't have noticed his terror. At the
moment, no ambition, no idea, no story—not even the exploits
of the Freedom Riders—could dissuade me from wanting this
HH to stay where he was, talking to me.

Hands as soft as cheese resting on the bar. A mystery—why
I thought saying yes once would build strength to say no later.
He had a new Pontiac the size of a boat, and that night, he said,
he wanted to drive me right up to Westchester to meet his parents. I told him it was already eight o'clock, but he didn't care.
His parents would be delighted. I got in the car with him and
thought that at least he would try to kiss me before meeting his
parents and that part would be exciting while also giving me
the excuse, later, to dismiss him. It took forty-five minutes by
highway and another half an hour over winding roads under
tall looming oaks and maples. The whole way he said nothing
about himself and only asked about me. Born in Long Island, an
only child. All this theater, I thought, the questions, the smooth
vinyl seats rolling over the gentle curves of the road through the
woods to the old stone house with the gravel drive—all because
he had liked the look of me from across the bar. He, she. His
hands, the car ride, my weight shifting around the curves, was a
seduction. A drug. I was swept forward into this gracious living
room with soft carpets and white sofas and hands bearing cups
of tea. His graying, bleary-eyed parents listened as he repeated
all that I had told him in the car. Everything he said suddenly
seemed like a fiction as I listened to my biography coming out of
his mouth (he had the dancing chin, too, of a teenager).

The parents insisted that we spend the night, in separate bedrooms, of course, mine the yellow room where the bed with its
cool sheets and down comforter and four mahogany posts felt
like a throne. Absolute silence reigned in the house, except for
the distant ticking of an old clock somewhere deep inside one of
the downstairs rooms, the heartbeat, I imagined, of a sentinel. I
slept better than I perhaps ever had before and waked to wain-
scotting scrubbed by sunlight showering through the shifting
leaves, the smell of coffee and bacon. Downstairs, someone had
sliced up a melon.

While all this happened, Charles Taylor, future president of Liberia, busied himself at Bentley College in Waltham, Massachusetts. While I ate melon in Westchester, Charles Taylor—on his way to killing thousands of Liberians and forcing thousands more into Zambia, where Bridget later met them at the Kuankan refugee camp—read *Wuthering Heights.*

Years later, when I first heard the story of what had happened to our daughter, I thought about the morning in the Hartman's house when I took that first bite of melon and knew I wouldn't attend graduate school in the fall or go down to Mississippi on a bus.

Our daughter, another woman, and two Kenyan doctors traveled near the Kuankan refugee camp in Guinea, close to the border with Liberia. As far as I understand, they drove right into a battle between two groups. Another truck with two armed men forced them off the road, shot the Zambian driver, Bridget's friend, and one of the doctors. The Guinean military opened fire and Bridget crawled into a ditch and covered her head. After it was over, the Guinean soldiers helped her to her feet and drove her back to Kuankan. At different times before and after, Bridget also worked in Liboi in Kenya on the Somalian border, and at Baduburran, forty-four kilometers west of Arcana, Ghana, exactly 4,965.7 miles from Carleton.

It didn't quite make sense that, as a consequence of giving up on myself—allowing myself to sink into what a therapist had called a "malaise" but I liked to call mayonnaise—I would become more selfish than I ever would have imagined. In Connecticut I sat in our house big enough for half a dozen children drinking glasses of wine and reading novels. I volunteered at the library and knew a few of the women there, but I never saw them outside the library. Bridget, who, by fourteen, had been sent to her father's boarding school in Massachusetts, seemed to think of nothing but other people's problems. Just like my parents. She came home in high school, when she came home, speaking of diasporas, legitimacy, "primitive time," apartheid, CIA conspiracies, commodification, the insidious recapitulation of patriarchal patterns of thought through the clear and seductive and ever-present stimulation of mass media—and sex, she said, looking at her mother, and heroin.

"Please tell me you have not been doing heroin," her father pleaded, "or having sex, for God's sake," and Bridget replied that her parents were completely obtuse, completely missing the point.

I didn't think I had missed the point. Every generation had to testify before their children, and in our case, the case of Hamilton and me, no real defense presented itself. We had essentially gone on a country drive and missed our whole lives. We had lived on scraps of the past, on his family's toilet money and my parents' virtue, and had done nothing ourselves. We had not loved each other or ourselves, but we loved Bridget—we both did, this the only reason we had tolerated each other as long as we had. In response, Bridget gave away the clothes I bought for her. She came home for holidays in rags she had found in trash bins. After college, she went to Guinea and watched strangers murder her friend, and then instead of coming to the states she went back to the camp and kept on working as if nothing had happened. She continued to attend to the thousands of victims of Charles Taylor, this man who had lived in a dorm at Bentley, eaten at the cafeteria, and probably read more than one Brontë novel, in a required literature seminar, and now oversaw the recruitment of child murderers and the hacking off of limbs and the raping of old women. In one case I had read about in the paper, soldiers forced a woman to march for miles carrying a bloody sack containing the heads of her children. On the other side of the border from this madman lived my daughter. Bridget had only ever given one answer to the question of why she stayed over there, so far from home: "I'm here because someone needs to do something about this misery." The kind of things my friends and I had once said to each other, before any of us had children of our own. I asked her if she wasn't just trying to do something about her own misery, but I got no answer.

Hamilton had coerced all the information about the incident that almost killed our daughter from someone at the UN. Bridget never told us the full story of what had happened in her own words. In a letter after the incident, she wrote that "people like us can choose to live happy lives, or we can choose to live meaningful lives." She had drawn the line, established the border. Bridget lived on one side, the meaningful side, while I lived on the other side.

When I moved to Maine for good, Bridget was still in boarding school. She came up for the winter holiday and stayed a week. Arming herself, then, for the important tasks that lay ahead, she was impatient to get back to school, which she endured so she could reach college, which she would endure until she could start her real life as far away from everyone she had known.

For the first two years of college, Bridget visited a couple days here and there in the winter and the summer and spent most of her time holed up in her bedroom at the back of the house. After her sophomore year, she stopped coming at all, and I had to drive down to see her. One day I arrived on campus, knocked on her door, and was met by some boy. Not her boyfriend, it turned out. Bridget had moved off campus somewhere. Unable to find her, I drove for hours back to Maine and on Monday called the college to find out where my daughter had moved, but they wouldn't give me the address over the phone.

"We can't be sure who you are," the woman, probably no more than a girl, explained. So I wrote to Bridget at her college

P.O. box and waited. A month later Bridget wrote back saying that she needed time to think about things.

Before she flew to Africa, she agreed to meet me. I drove down to Boston and met her at a café. She remained stern and quiet for the first half an hour. I knew she'd rushed through college and graduated early with no ceremony. I talked about my job at the library while she stared into her coffee and ground her jaw. Finally, she lifted her face and began speaking, at first with her eyes closed and then with her eyes open, unblinking and jumpy. Over the years I have translated her words into my own words so that when I think of the speech I hear my own voice: I had thought only of myself, had forgotten to pick her up at school, missed conferences with teachers, didn't even clean my own house or cook half the time, never worked, had no real friends, and the drinking, the horrible, silent, sitting at the kitchen table drinking from a bottomless wine glass in the barren tomb of the seven-bedroom house made for six children but for which only one child had been provided by the barren wife.

"Thank God," she said, "only one child."

Bridget had never, ever, in my memory said the word God before. "Thank God there were no more children in that house to go through what I went through." Of course, Bridget was saying just the opposite: it would have been a sad thing to grow up in that big house with those empty rooms as reminders of her loneliness.

I refrained from pointing out that people often said the opposite of what they meant, especially when they were not aware of it. In fact, I might have added, people were often also the opposite of how they thought of themselves. People were also the lives they might have led, which was why, I might have said, I was not giving up. At that moment, I might have mentioned what the doctors had just told me about the cancer in my abdomen. I should have been in the hospital instead of driving for hours for a cup of coffee. I might have said goodbye forever when Bridget stood up to go, her jaw set on a course to save Africa by annihilating herself. I might have offered one word in defense of myself, of my years as a mother. I had always loved my daughter, but of course, you couldn't offer a word—or a feeling—in defense of what you had or had not done.

I had received a death sentence from the doctors (thirty percent chance of survival). But I would keep going because that's what people did. They walked around inside an outline of a life. The outline would continue with a life of its own: Janet Hartman, 341 Washington Street, Carleton, Maine.

"I will always be your mother," I said to Bridget.

And then Bridget walked away.

As I went through the motions of my treatment, I frequently tried to imagine the camp where Bridget worked. The overwhelming despair. Could you really help people, I wondered, if you were there to extinguish yourself with other people's misery? Motives didn't matter, maybe, when the misery was so basic in nature, where people were dying.

I wondered what I would have found in Mississippi in the 1960s. During my marriage, my husband left before six in the morning and often came back after eight p.m. at night, usually six days a week. Bridget would see him half of Sunday if he played golf. Yet I supposed it was natural that Bridget let him off without a trial. I was the one sitting at the kitchen table when Bridget woke every morning and when she came home from school gripping her backpack and ripe banana too tightly. The veins stood out on her hands and on her skinny neck. For years she looked at me with what seemed like so much need that I began to think of her not as one person but as a representative of a people.

When she was young, I had always stroked her hair as she fell asleep—I wanted to wrap my arms around her and draw her close. The smell of her neck, the pale skin of her inner arm, the perfect cursive of her reports for school. I wanted to step where she stepped with those sapling legs springing through the backyard. Yet so often I stayed at the kitchen table and drank, and when I did pick Bridget up at school instead of letting her take the bus home, I felt paralyzed by the sight of all those kids— the army—on the other side of the fence chasing and running and swinging and kicking. So many of them, and they needed so much.

After my illness, I thought of her waking in a tent or a cinderblock building and walking into the stifling air among the thousands of people, many of them children, who had come to this place because they needed help. After seeing her friend murdered (her face shot, Hamilton learned after calling a journalist in London), Bridget might bolt awake every morning with terror. Yet she kept doing what she had been doing, arranging for medical visits. Food distribution (what else, I didn't know).

Over the years, I wrote Bridget a letter once a week, sent her packages once a month. I got up every day and did the things I had set out to do to give her courage—to help her keep going. Maybe there was no truth to this—a harmless lie, but a lie nonetheless. Maybe nothing connected us.

After the illness, I went back to working at the library, volunteering at the school, volunteering with hospice bringing meals to people who were dying. I washed the sheets in Bridget's bedroom every two months. The sheets were never slept in, the letters to her never answered, the kids I read to at the school mostly stared straight ahead waiting for it to be over, the people I brought meals to, many of them childless and in pain, wanted things to hurry along. They wanted it to be over. Many if not most days I wanted the same thing: to give up. Yet I went on in this place where most people's families had lived for generations, where they tolerated me but didn't need me. People here at the school, the library, the hospital, didn't look at me with the craving and desperation that I remembered seeing in Bridget's eyes when she was a child. I had come to the habit of love a little too late for the world—or for Bridget—to come to the habit of noticing.

I met him in the grocery store, back when Bridget was seven. A young guy in a T-shirt who started joking with me about a tabloid, which claimed that some senator seen with a supermodel would soon leave his wife. I didn't know why, but I asked him what he did. I had never done this before, not even when I was single, and when he said he was a music teacher, I said, without missing a beat, that I had been looking for a music teacher for my daughter. I didn't mention my husband, only that I had a child. As I walked out to the car with him, I kept my wedding ring hidden in the folds of my dress. The first lie led to a second and a third: the previous music teacher had broken his arm, my daughter loved to play the piano. I had assumed he taught piano, but maybe he didn't, so I said my daughter wanted to try other instruments. Each story I told necessitated another. When the man came to the house, to meet Bridget to see about the lessons (he did play the piano), I claimed that Bridget's schedule had changed for the day. After getting him a drink, I began to tell him that my husband had been having an affair for half a year when of course Hamilton had done no such thing and would do no such thing. This lie spontaneously produced tears in my eyes. As Timmy—that was his name—began to comfort me, I even felt outraged at my husband's fictional infidelity. I experienced true vengeance as I kissed Timmy, and later felt justified as I made up stories to tell Hamilton about where I sometimes went in the evenings and weekends. I hated myself for what I was doing as much as I hated myself for the lack of originality.

I'd spent thousands of dollars talking to a therapist about why I had married my husband—therapists never quite give you a way out. The whole time the answer was simple: a safe option in life presented itself. A rich, stable man. All I had to do was say yes and the difficulties, trials, uncertainties, and challenges of my future would cease to be a problem.

One day Timmy and I were in the middle of it in my bedroom when the door flew open and there was Bridget with her backpack. I was on all fours with Timmy behind me. Timmy scooted away and ran out of the room. Bridget just stood there for minutes while her mother dressed.

That night, during the usual late super after Hamilton arrived home, Bridget wouldn't eat her food. Hamilton asked her what was wrong.

"I saw Mom naked with a man in the bedroom today."

Bridget glared at me, her eyes filled with tears.

I sighed. "She's angry with me because I won't let her spend the weekend at the Spurlings next weekend."

Hamilton stopped chewing and looked from me to Bridget and back again.

"Why won't you let her spend the night at the Spurlings?" he asked.

"Because it's your father's birthday next weekend and we're going down to Southampton." I momentarily felt uncertain about what was true and not true.

"That's right," Hamilton muttered. It was true that Bridget and I had not been getting along for more than a year. Bridget always went to her father if she wanted to hear yes. She had never made this kind of claim before, though, and I couldn't tell what Hamilton believed.

"I don't want to spend the night at the Spurlings," Bridget protested. "I never did."

"Of course not," I said. "It's your grandfather's birthday. And it is not acceptable for you to make up horrible stories like that about your mother. Do you hear me, young lady?"

I heard the words come out of my mouth. I would say anything. I was outside myself, looming over myself in a state of shock, but these were my words. No one else's. I watched as the gears turned behind Bridget's eyes. She slumped in her seat and looked as exhausted as a ninety-year-old.

"No, you can't go to the Spurlings next weekend," Hamilton said, taking another bite of his asparagus. "You can go the weekend after."

When I found out I was sick, it seemed fitting that my cells had started metastasizing while I had been having sex in the reading room with Tony, the head librarian—my second affair, this one at least as a single woman. Nothing good could come of having sex with your boss (someone else's husband, a boy-man in the body of a plucked seagull) in a public library where children read *Stuart Little* and former shop stewards thumbed through *Popular Mechanics*. Tony clearly wanted me from the first day we met. I knew this from the way he pursed his lips and pinched his brow, just slightly. For some men, constipation and sexual frustration look exactly the same. I let him do it once standing up while I stared at the cover of *Architectural Digest*, a magazine I had never bothered to pick up before. Architecture was a subject for people who thought the world made sense.

The first casualty of the problem with my body, the rhythm of my habits: I forgot my volunteer work with Meals on Wheels and hospice, I forgot to show up at the school, I stopped walking. I had started thinking of smoking again for the first time in years. When I found out the cause of the pain in my stomach, I called my ex-husband, Hamilton, I didn't know why, except the fear that no one else would care. No parents, siblings, no one but a second cousin whom I hadn't seen since the first grade. Hamilton became the boy I had known when we first met. He wanted me to stay with him, with him and Amanda, his new wife, and he would arrange everything for me at Sloane. I said no, I would be fine with the hospital in Portland and in Carleton. I had just wanted to tell one person who had known me. He agreed not to drive up and not to tell Bridget. I reserved the right to tell our daughter.

After I started the treatments, I returned home in the afternoons. Sally from hospice stopped by the house to see if I wanted to keep volunteering. It was helpful to know instead of having the volunteer not show up. "I don't know," I told her, "I'm dying so you better take me off the volunteer list and put me on another list." Then two people outside the hospital knew. Sally looked as if I had flashed her (I'm afraid I often have this effect on people), then she looked like a child whose cat had been found crushed by a station wagon. The stages of someone else's second-hand grief. So much for telling other people about my problems.

Calls came in from the school and from Laurie, the woman who had brought yoga to Carleton the year before. Laurie suggested more yoga and wheatgrass instead of chemo. After the first week of chemo, a letter arrived from Tony at the library announcing that I had been let go. I didn't think too much of it at the time. My main concern, the only thing I could think about then, saying goodbye to my daughter, took the place of all other worries. I couldn't bear the thought of other people's pity, especially Bridget's. I turned the volume down on the phone ringer. Hamilton called every couple of days. The loyal soldier. I had started to lie to him, telling him everything looked good. At that stage, I woke up every morning completely exhausted, and I had lost my sense of smell.

One day I rose late, at ten, and realizing I had missed the chemo poisoning for that day, sentenced myself to the kitchen table in my robe while I waited for the coffee to brew. I would drink the coffee and call the nurses and tell them what? I didn't know. *See you tomorrow.* I would have ignored the knock at the door except that I could see Corson holding a paper bag through the window.

"I heard you were sick," Corson said bluntly when I opened the door.

"Who told you that?"

"Charlotte came in with her kid. She told me."

Surely even in Carleton the hospital had rules about what nurses could reveal, but I didn't really care. Corson shrugged and kept standing there. "I've got a whole mess of things my Grandma made. Not sure you want them if you're sick. Biscuits and jam and a pie."

"That's very kind of you," I said.

"I didn't make it," Corson said, looking down at the bag.

"Do other people know, do you think?"

Corson raised an eyebrow. "I don't know what other people know," he said, still standing in the doorway. I offered him tea. "Oh, no, don't go to the trouble," Corson said. He set the bag down on the table but didn't sit. Corson and I had worked together for only a short time at that point. He was laconic in the extreme and never revealed much.

He returned the next day with some kind of fish stew and again would not sit down for tea but scurried out the door as soon as he could. I couldn't understand why Corson's grandmother went to so much trouble until I remembered the time a few years before when I heard Corson asking Tony for just a few hours off because his grandfather had to go into the hospital. I offered to drive them because I knew Corson's family no longer had a car. Corson thanked me but said that his grandfather didn't feel so bad that he couldn't walk, especially in the morning. I showed up at the apartment anyway and said I was just driving by on my way to Bracket's. Corson's grandfather didn't look as though he could walk across the room, let alone across town to the hospital. The man couldn't have weighed more than eighty-five pounds. I suspected that drink had aged him. Corson stood on his right side, the grandmother on his left, and they lifted him to his feet. I couldn't tell from looking at the grandfather's glazed eyes if he knew whether he was standing or sleeping.

I went back to the poison after two missed days, and Corson arrived late every afternoon, bringing me biscuits and jam or bread or some fish concoction, usually mixed with beets and potatoes. One day before Corson showed up, I looked in the mirror and noticed my hair thinning. Even though I knew he would arrive any moment, I found paper scissors in the upstairs closet and started cutting my hair off in patches next to my scalp. When the knock sounded at the door, I thought about not answering.

"What happened to your head?" Corson asked right away when I opened the door.

I turned and took my seat at the table. Corson set his latest round of goods on the counter, put on the kettle, picked the scissors off the floor where I'd dropped them, and for a few moments just stood behind me. Before the kettle boiled, Corson, making a strange humming noise as he worked, as if he were alone, started to chop at my hair. He paused to make the tea, and, still humming, kept on with his snipping. Occasionally, he gripped my head and tilted me left or right. He made his fingers into a comb and ran them down along my scalp. I felt the muscles along my jaw and in my face give way.

When he had finished, Corson sat down to drink his tea as if nothing unusual had happened. I wiped my face with my sleeve.

I still don't think we were friends at this point, not yet. Even when he stood right next to me, Corson was far away. I often thought of the island where he had lived. Aside from his grandmother, he never saw the other people on the island after they left when he was twelve. As far as I could tell, one day he was living in the nineteenth century, and the next he was living here in the shadow of the Carleton Ironworks. Carleton High School, where he was a student, was five times the size of the island population where he had once lived. As we sat in the kitchen together, I asked how long it had been exactly since his family had left the island.

"Couple years, I guess," Corson said.

"I thought it was longer than that."

"I'll be going back to the island soon," Corson said. "My grandma and I are going to run a ferryboat out from Dennis to some of the islands for tourists. We might run people over to Nova Scotia for a price." He spoke in a low voice, as if afraid someone else would hear.

I thought of Corson's grandmother, her hands permanently curled into claws. She seemed barely strong enough to carry a grocery bag. And Corson, not old enough to have a driver's license, could certainly not operate a ferryboat.

"We'll put in a hauler so we can fish, too."

Corson had delivered his entire plan. Now his eyelids snapped shut and tightened like bottle caps.

"People like the puffins," he added. I wondered if he was about to cry. "They'll pay ten dollars to go out and see a puffin. Even in the fog."

"That's good money," I said, and Corson nodded solemnly, a little pleased, it seemed. "They taste like mice," Corson said with authority.

"What does? Puffin?"

Corson laughed. "Don't tell Tony about what I said. About going back to the island."

"I would not tell Tony, believe me."

"I don't want anyone to know."

Corson leaned forward. I did also, even though it hurt my insides to do so.

"We all know you and Tony were together. I hear everyone talking about it."

"What do they say?"

"They say poor Carol. That's his wife."

"Yes, I know who she is."

"And they say you're a terrible person." Corson's lips pulled tight across his mouth.

"Well, they would."

"But you're not. You just made a mistake.... But not as bad a mistake, if you ask me, as marrying him."

"Yes," I said. "It was a mistake, and I would agree with you—not as bad a mistake as marrying him."

"People should be angry at Carol for marrying him."

"That's an interesting point of view."

"That's the way it is." Corson shrugged.

"I'm dying," I said to the floor.

"You don't look like someone who's dying," Corson said flatly.

There I was, bald as a vulture, surrounded by my fallen hair, and losing weight faster than a punctured balloon. I started to laugh so hard I thought I might throw up.

"What?" Corson said, obviously confused.

To my surprise, I didn't die. I resumed walking in the mornings. The school, hospice, my old job back. I kept going. Time kept moving forward, but also in circles.

On the morning when Bridget was to arrive by bus, Saturday morning—barely a week since Corson's grandmother had died—I went shopping for groceries. I had no idea what kind of food she ate now. She lived in a place where there wasn't enough food. Usually, there was a man in a wheelchair who ate breakfast at Bracket's who wanted to tell me all about the brother who wouldn't answer his calls. Sometimes I chatted with the woman, married to an alcoholic welder, who worked in the stockroom and went to the First Baptist. For some reason, the woman thought I was a Baptist, too. Also, I often ran across the two old veterans who wanted to know what kind of books people checked out at the library. They were convinced, they told me, that Communists had infiltrated the town and wanted to study how to make a bomb.

I was supposed to pick Corson up at his grandmother's apartment, but I was having trouble remembering how to cross town. I wasn't even that old at this point. Not compared to the age I am now. Despite the bright sun on Centre Street, when I stopped at the light, I could see through the plate glass store window of Gediman's to all the new washing machines and refrigerators and stoves. Gediman stood with his hand on top of a dryer and spoke to a woman and her child. They only sold General Electric. In case you weren't sure, a sign on the door told you so. Whenever I saw Mr. Gediman in the library, I thought of Corson's grandfather, who, when he could no longer work, would wander over to Gediman's for a couple hours before stopping by the library to pick Corson up at the end of his shift. He liked to say that old Gediman had something up his sleeve besides his arm. He would go on about how a person would have to be foolish to buy a Maytag or a Frigidaire rather than a General Electric appliance.

When his grandfather fell ill, sometimes Corson spent a few hours sitting in the reading room after his work had ended. I suspected that he didn't want to see the pain in his grandfather's face.

At the stop sign by Reny's, I really was confused about which way to go. Because there was no one behind me, I just sat there looking up at the second-story window above Reny's and spotted Marie, the woman with the Quebec patois, peering out the window of her apartment. Marie's gone now, so I suppose it's okay to state what everyone knew: she stole people's change when she cleaned their houses. Still, she was the most thorough cleaner in town, and also the cheapest, even accounting for what she took, never more than five dollars. When she cleaned for me, I always paid her to clean Bridget's room, even though no one had stayed there in several years. Every two weeks, Marie changed the sheets. The quilt on the bed was the same as the one Bridget had as a girl. Some of her stuffed animals sat on the bureau against one wall. A watercolor she had made in sixth grade was framed above the bed.

Above Marie's apartment, the sky cracked open like a mussel and silver dissolved into blue-black. In moments, the wind flicked cold rain against the windshield. I have no idea how long I was stopped there. Eventually, as you can imagine, someone beeped at me, and I took a right. Corson was standing in front of his apartment (it was solely his now) with his arms hanging at his sides. I rolled down the window and told him I had donuts in the backseat. He loved the Bracket's donuts, which I tried to avoid because my yoga teacher called them "cancer food." I had already eaten two sitting in the Bracket's parking lot.

"I'm feeling glazed," I said as he slid into the car.

In Brunswick, I pulled into the 7-11 lot and parked. On the other side of the walkway stood a rusty bench with no overhang. The bus stop. I wondered what would happen if I didn't recognize my own daughter. I hadn't seen pictures of her or heard her voice in a long time.

"I don't like Brunswick," I mumbled. The strip of gas stations and convenience stores. With my fingers still gripping the top of the steering wheel, I glared at the bench. "It's the beginning of Portland."

"I thought you liked Portland," Corson said.

"That was last year. I'm changeable. I guess you don't know that."

"I do," Corson said matter-of-factly.

"Do you want a Diet Coke?" I asked, pointing toward the 7-11. Corson looked surprised. It was true; I never ate junk food at work and now I was following up donuts with Coke. In the store, I dropped the Coke and a Mars Bar on the counter; the Coke almost rolled off. The teenager in the uniform seemed to be rolling his eyes without actually rolling his eyes.

"Just ring me up," I said to him.

"Sure, lady," and now he did roll his eyes.

By the time I reached the car, I'd swallowed half the bottle. My eyeballs felt squeezed and jumpy in the morning light.

I heard the diesel engine of the bus before I spotted it rounding the corner. The driver geared down and stopped. When the hydraulic door slid aside, two feet descended the metal steps. Two boots, two pant legs, a man with a paper bag neatly rolled at the top, and no one else stepped into the light. I didn't know how long I'd been holding my breath when I finally exhaled.

"I'm sorry," Corson said.

"No, it's fine," I said, my voice rising more from the caffeine than emotion. "I didn't really think she would come." The words seemed to have been spoken by someone outside the car. I poured the rest of the Coke out the window and threw the bottle into the backseat.

"When Bridget was young," I said, "while I was still married, I had an affair with someone, and she caught us." The confession sounded so anticlimactic because this was only the banal part of the betrayal. The rest was unfathomable and extended down into the roots of our lives. Bridget and I had never discussed any of it. I could stand the guilt, I could even stand not seeing her or hearing her voice, but what I could barely survive month to month, day to day, and sometimes moment to moment, was not knowing if she was even alive. These were the hardest years of my life, before she did finally move home for good and settle down a day's drive from here and we began to talk again.

"That was a long time ago," Corson said, as if it was a story he'd heard many times before.

"Yes, and no," I said and started the car. Instead of taking Route One, I chose the slow way and drove half the speed limit down the Old Carleton Road, the only way to Carleton before they built the highway. Though I'd known all along that Bridget wouldn't be on that bus, I still felt my heart pounding in my temples.

"What am I going to do now?" Corson said and turned to face me, his eyebrows knit together. I was spinning inside and didn't have an answer for him right away. He was only seventeen, and now that his grandmother was dead, he wouldn't be allowed to stay alone. In a few weeks, his mother would fly back from Alaska for a short visit and to scatter her mother's ashes. I'd met her several times before. She and I would have a long talk. She'd see the wisdom of what I would propose—that Corson stay with me until he finished high school.

Corson would move into Bridget's room. In the end, he stayed for more than three years, and he became my family. When he was ready, I drove him around the region to visit colleges until he found one where he thought he might be happy for a few years, which he was, I think. I helped him as much as I could. After he graduated, he came back to Carleton and moved up the street from me. Eventually, he bought a house at the edge of town. He never married, something we never discussed. He had a friend who lived in Calais, whom he visited once a month or so. I was sad that I never met this friend, who has since passed away, never even knew the friend's name, but I accepted it. We shared so much, and this was a part of his life he kept separate.

Of course, it's always impossible to know what lies ahead. That morning, after Bridget didn't arrive by bus, we passed the Sunoco Station and the UShip Store as large raindrops fell against the windshield and ran together in streams across the glass. We turned onto School Street and took a left onto the section of Washington Street lined with churches and ship captain's houses. Up the hill, we passed the library where we both worked. By the time I pulled into the driveway in front of the green clapboard house my ex-husband had bought so many years before, I felt as if I had driven nonstop across the country. My hands were glued to the steering wheel. Sheets of rain curved out of the sky. I couldn't remember if I'd left the kitchen window open and couldn't bear the thought of finding the floors flooded. Corson said nothing for several minutes. Then he stepped out of the car, walked around to my side, and opened the door. I swung my feet onto the pavement and started to walk, but halfway up the steps, I stopped and raised my face. Though I wasn't confident that we would figure everything out, I told Corson that we would. Maybe he believed me, maybe he simply felt relieved that someone cared enough to make a promise they might not be able to keep. His face relaxed and he took a deep breath. First, I told him, we'd better get inside, build a fire in the woodstove, and boil water for tea. It would take a full day of cooking and wandering from room to room for the house to feel like a place where people lived.

Acknowledgments

I WISH TO THANK the following people, institutions, and books: Nicola Fucigna, Isabel Fucigna, Nathan Harris, George Smith, Keith Scribner, Marjorie Celona, Brian Trapp, Kirstin Valdez Quade, Jamie Poissant, Cary Groner, Mat Johnson, Dylan Willoughby, Mara Brandsdorfer, Julia Sippel, The University of Oregon, *New England Captives Carried to Canada Between 1677 and 1760 During the French and Indian Wars* by Emma Lewis Coleman (1926), *The Dalhousie Review* (first published "Emily's Story: from the Journal of Emily Wills, 1810-1815" in slightly different form), and Colin Sargent at *Portland Monthly Magazine* (first published a short excerpt called "Outermark").

JASON BROWN is the author of three books of short stories: *Driving the Heart and Other Stories* (Norton/Random House), *Why the Devil Chose New England for His Work* (Open City/Grove Atlantic), and *A Faithful but Melancholy Account of Several Barbarities Lately Committed* (Missouri Review Books), winner of the Maine book award. His stories and essays have appeared in *Best American Short Stories*, *The New Yorker*, *Best American Essays*, *The Atlantic*, *Harper's*, *The Pushcart Prize Anthology*, among others. Brown grew up in Maine, earned his BA from Bowdoin College, his MFA from Cornell University, and was a Stegner Fellow and Truman Capote Fellow at Stanford University. He has lived on several Maine islands and in Cape Breton, Nova Scotia. After teaching for many years at the University of Arizona, he now teaches in the MFA program at the University of Oregon, and lives in Eugene, OR and in MidCoast Maine.